DARK AS MY HEART

ANTTI TUOMAINEN

TRANSLATED FROM THE FINNISH BY LOLA ROGERS

LARGE
PRINT

First published in Great Britain 2015
by
Harvill Secker

First Isis Edition
published 2016
by arrangement with
Harvill Secker
Penguin Random House

A catalogue record for this book is available
from the British Library.

ISBN 978–1–78541–187–8 (hb)
ISBN 978–1–78541–193–9 (pb)

Published by
F. A. Thorpe (Publishing)
Anstey, Leicestershire

Set by Words & Graphics Ltd.
Anstey, Leicestershire
Printed and bound in Great Britain by
T. J. International Ltd., Padstow, Cornwall

This book is printed on acid-free paper

For my mother

I sang to my dear dead mother
and she instantly understood me,
and pressing a kiss to my forehead said
as into her arms she pulled me:
"Believe then in truth, or in fantasy, —
if you'll only believe in it utterly!
For truth is what you believe it to be.
My son, believe in your dreams!"

EINO LEINO, "Smiling Apollo"

THE BEGINNING

She'd met a man and now her mouth was filling with blood. These things were connected, and yet not connected.

What had she done wrong?

Nothing she could think of.

And yet . . .

Her chin stung on one side, the crushed outer fingers of her left hand cried out in pain, and it seemed there was worse to come.

It was incredible how quickly her mind was flying, the things it found, the things it saw and remembered.

A year earlier her life had changed completely. No, not completely. It changed completely thirteen years ago, when her son was born. But over the past year her life had opened up, as if a piece of paper wadded in her fist had been smoothed flat, as if a storm had moved on and the sun had risen after years below the horizon.

She'd heard that in moments of great distress you don't really feel distressed, that at the moment of death or intense panic or shock, you don't realise you're going to die. It wasn't true, of course. She was thinking with a level of clarity she'd seldom experienced before.

She even saw how beautiful everything was, everything on either side of the long, gleaming knife. Her son. Her life. In that order.

The brilliance of that thought lit up the inside of the car, its cramped and airless space tinted a feverish artificial green by the dashboard lights, as if they were in a submarine sinking for miles into deep water. But the thought didn't remain submerged in the car. It lit up the creeping October evening outside, the thick grey veil of rain like a mist, but wetter, and freezing cold. She saw all of her thirty-two years, and she knew what was important and what wasn't.

If there had been time, she might have laughed. If there had been time, she might have thought — practical and optimistic as she was — that things could be worse. That she could have raced through her life without understanding its beauty, without seeing the wonders before her, all around her. She could have been, even now, absorbed in some inessential thing.

Instead she was fending off a knife with her hand.

The long, steel blade pierced her skin again. Her hand, narrow and delicate. The knife broad and cold. It went through her palm and into her wrist.

She said to herself again that this was happening because she'd met a man, befriended him.

She said this to herself many times. The truth of it was shocking. She'd met a man, she was fending off a knife. There could hardly have been a greater incongruity between the two, and yet the first thing led to the second. To this. She remembered an American movie where a tired policeman was trying to sum up the nature of life to his younger colleague. Anything can happen to anyone at any time, he said.

I guess so.

But still.

She thought about her son again. There were suddenly so many things she ought to talk to him about. They started to trample over each other, crowd each other out, tumbling and clashing and tripping in their rush.

Her son. He should at least know . . .

How much she loved him . . .

That required sacrifice.

She had to reach her hand further. That made her chest and stomach vulnerable to the swiftly swinging knife.

She lunged forward as far as the safety belt would let her. How ironic that they called it a safety belt.

Her hand got hold of something, her fingernails scratched. She scratched the side of a neck, dug her nails as deep as she could with the strength she had left. She was sure that her nails were piercing flesh, sure that she felt blood and muscle under her fingers.

This had a price. She had opened her arms. The knife struck her chest.

Her strength was running out. She couldn't feel her hands any more. A moment later she realised that they were in her lap, saw that under her fingernails — the nails that weren't broken, the fingers that weren't broken — there was skin and blood that was a different colour to her own.

That was something.

The knife stopped swinging.

The car moved.

She realised that she wasn't holding her breath. She just couldn't breathe.

She wanted to get out of the car. She thought — clearly, lucidly — that she had to get away, had to make herself get away.

And at that moment she felt as if she was flying, rushing towards the warmest, friendliest of suns.

It seemed her wish was coming true.

She was flying to her son.

TWENTY YEARS LATER

SEPTEMBER 2013

In other circumstances, at some other time, I would already have made my move.

I knew myself.

She was slim, her hair black and shining, thickly draped over her shoulders and down her back, her fringe short enough to show her sharply drawn brows. Against her pale, almost white skin, her hair was like raven's feathers scattered over pure drifts of snow. The same impenetrable black continued in her long, languid lashes, and in the centre of it all her blue-grey eyes gazed at me unrelentingly.

Her expression was a mixture of calm, secure superiority, and something else that I couldn't quite put my finger on at this first meeting. To do that would have required that I get up from the dark brown leather armchair, walk around the oval table of antique walnut, and sit down next to her on the overstuffed, pale gold sofa. That was something I didn't intend to do, for lots of reasons.

The first reason had to do with who she was. Her name was Amanda Saarinen and she was just setting a glass of wine down on the table. On the rim of the glass was a smudge of dark red lipstick the length and width of a little finger.

"You're the new caretaker."

The top three buttons of her black, wide-collared blouse were undone. I had already noticed that she was a devotee of plastic surgery. There was something in the result that matched the faux antique sofa she was sitting on. The flower arrangement on the table repeated the pale yellow and orange of the flowers and coats of arms in the wallpaper that spread behind her in both directions. She looked as if she was posed in a painting.

"You don't look like a caretaker," she said, reaching a hand over the table. "I forgot to introduce myself. Amanda Saarinen."

"That's all right. Aleksi Kivi," I said, squeezing her hand and sitting down again. "I guessed you were Amanda. I've only been here for a week. Maybe I'll eventually start to look like a caretaker."

She almost smiled. She was thirty-one, two years younger than me. She picked up her glass of wine again. It was eleven-thirty in the morning.

"Maintenance men are short, stocky, overgrown boys in their fifties. They wear cargo pants and belts with a hundred and fifty different keys and a Leatherman and one of those mobile phones you can use underwater. They don't listen when you talk to them. You seem to be listening to what I'm saying. How can that be?"

"I *am* listening."

"And your fingernails are clean. Very un-caretaker-like."

8

She took a sip of wine.

"And you really want to work here?"

"Yes."

"Why?"

"For a change."

Amanda looked at me.

"Sure, but a change to what?"

"Well, the renovation, for one thing. I'm a carpenter by trade and I've worked as one for almost ten years. Mostly renovations. I wanted a change to just one project. To be able to take my time and focus, do things the way they should be done."

That last part was true. Not the whole truth, but true all the same.

"I'd like to find something I want to do, too."

"I think that time comes when it comes."

"I think that time's already past."

I didn't say anything.

"What else?" she asked. "You've been a carpenter. Anything else?"

"Not much else. I ran a second-hand bookshop for a little over a year in Kallio, near the park. It didn't work at all. I sold the books too cheap because I wanted people to read them."

"Interesting," Amanda said, not sounding terribly sincere.

She took another sip of wine. There was just a drop left at the bottom.

"What did they tell you about this place?" she asked.

"That it's important to the family, more of a refuge than a residence."

"I guess you could say that. Did they tell you anything about a woman in her thirties practically living here who no longer has a single friend?"

I looked at her.

"I find that hard to believe."

"Hard to believe that somebody is hiding herself away here, or hard to believe she has no friends?"

"Both. But then, it's none of my business."

"I guess not," she said quietly.

We were sitting in front of glass-paned double doors. The white of the door and window frames was fresh, just painted. Outside the windows a bright and cloudless, windy early September day made the oak and maple leaves jangle yellow, gold and rich red. Beyond the trees the sparkling sea spread to the horizon. Over it all lay a cobalt blue sky. It was nearly impossible to imagine the dark coldness of space beyond it, but it was there. Of course it was.

Amanda seemed to have forgotten that I existed. She stared out at the garden, or the sea, her expression fixed. I remembered Miia again, which made me think of what I'd once had, and what I'd left behind to come here and do what I had to do.

I looked around. They called this the hall. A good name for seventy square metres of space, the largest room in the manor. The understated wallpaper was bordered by waist-high grey wainscoting. From the ceiling hung two identical crystal chandeliers that hadn't been lit once in the week I'd been at the house.

Although I hadn't actually been in the house. I had my own small room and kitchen at one end of an outbuilding.

"Have you met him?" Amanda asked.

"Who?"

"My father, of course."

Of course.

"No."

Something flashed in her eyes.

"What about Markus?"

"Markus . . ."

"Yes, Markus Harmala, my father's chauffeur."

"No. Why would he be here when Henrik isn't?"

She didn't bother to answer that question. She stared me straight in the eye.

"How many times did they interview you?" she asked.

"Three times."

"Does that include those silly psychological tests?"

"They weren't silly. But it's four, if you count the tests."

"My father just wants to be sure, I guess," she said, not sounding particularly convinced. She picked up her empty glass, looked at it for a moment, then raised her eyes again.

"What were you doing when I sent for you?"

"I was on my way downstairs to check how much water is being used, since they installed the new . . ."

"Right. You've got to get back to work. Naturally. I was just leaving anyway. Did I leave my car outside?"

"Yes, you did," I said. "If that black Range Rover is yours. It's right in front of the door."

Amanda read my thoughts.

"One glass of wine," she said with a smile. "I'm all right to drive."

I saw no reason to argue with her. She got up from the sofa and pulled on her coat, and I did the same. I followed her out. The wind took hold of my hair and chilled my skin, which had grown warm, almost feverish, while I was indoors. Amanda walked with purposeful steps. Somewhere nearby the last blackbird of autumn sang. We went to her car.

"I wanted to meet you," Amanda said. "It's no trivial matter to me who is here taking care of the place. For many reasons."

"I understand," I said.

We stood less than a metre apart. Up close, Amanda's eyes were hard and shiny. The wind fluttered her black hair over her face. When it blew the right way I caught a whiff of alcohol in the air.

"See you later," she said, and in one smooth movement was in her car.

The Range Rover skidded over the deep brown ruts in the gravel. It disappeared into the birch woods and I took a deep breath of cleansing air, literally breathing a sigh of relief.

In other circumstances, at some other time.

Maybe.

But not now.

The police had rung the doorbell as I was standing in front of the television eating Weetabix. The television was on, but I wasn't watching it.

They'd said their names, said they were from the criminal division, and asked if they could come in. I didn't say anything. I was thirteen years old and my mouth was full of cold skimmed milk and mushy cereal.

They didn't wait for me to swallow. They stepped inside and walked to the living room. They asked me to sit down.

They were wearing suits and skinny ties with loosened knots. They looked at me with sad faces. They had blue and purple bags under their eyes, swollen and heavy. When we'd sat for a moment in silence they asked whether I had any close relatives they could call.

My mother, I said.

Anyone else, one of them asked. He had yellow teeth.

I shook my head.

Your father, the other one asked. He had the longest, shiniest forehead I'd ever seen.

I shook my head.

An aunt? Uncle? Grandma? Grandpa?

No. It was just my mother and me. We didn't need anything else.

I'll call social services, the yellow teeth said to the shiny forehead, and got up and went into the kitchen to use the phone.

I sat silently with the shiny forehead. The yellow teeth murmured on the other side of the wall. He came back and nodded to his companion. The one with the shiny forehead cleared his throat, although there was nothing in it to clear.

Your mother is missing, he said.

No, she's not, I said.

There was a sharp taste of acid and warm milk in my mouth.

We're going to take you with us. We need to talk.

At the police station a woman wearing a blue scarf around her neck sat beside me. Other than the scarf she was completely white. Her face, hair, and clothes were various shades of white. Now and then she put her hand on my shoulder. It felt strange. It wasn't my mother's hand.

The police asked her if they could continue asking me questions. The woman asked me if I was getting tired.

I said I wasn't. I wanted my mother back.

All of the questions were about her.

What had our life been like recently?

Had she met anyone?

Did she have a boyfriend?

She hadn't been threatened by anyone?

Had I seen any men around her?

Did I know anything about the men?

Had my mother been happy? Normal? Cheerful? Sad?

What had she been wearing that morning? What did she say before she left for work? How did she say what she said? Did she ever talk about people she was going to see? If so, did I remember anyone in particular?

And so on.

Weeks went by. The policemen changed but the questions were the same.

Months went by, and although the questions were the same, they came less frequently. Then they stopped altogether.

I was thirteen years old.

I knew that the police would never figure out where my mother had gone.

I still knew it.

Kalmela Manor stood on the seashore ninety-four kilometres west of Helsinki, in a spot that had been thought desirable in 1850. The estate covered a hundred and sixteen hectares, less than half of it farmland. The rest was forest, both wild and cultivated. The shoreline was a kilometre long, with a little more than a tenth of it, about a hundred and twenty metres of the eastern half, clear cut. From the long dock to the west you could see hundreds of metres of rocks and thickets broken up by at least two steep, red-grey stone cliffs.

The manor was built on a spot where the ground rose above the surrounding landscape. The house at the top of the hill dominated its surroundings and looked as large and yellow as the sun on a cloudless day. The other buildings included the outbuilding with its garage, the guest house, a boat shed, and a seaside sauna.

The farm fields were rented to locals. In September they lay bare and stubbled and, depending on the clearness of the day and the position of the sun, could appear golden-yellow, tired brown, or grey as wool felt.

In the spring they would again sprout rye, oats, sugar beets, and potatoes.

There was plentiful forest in every direction, surprisingly dark and dense even in autumn.

The main building had been renovated at the turn of the millennium. It was an assortment of pale yellows beautifully complemented by the white of window frames and pillars as thick as punchbags flanking the entrance. There were two floors, eight rooms, and a professional kitchen. Downstairs was the common space. It was dominated by the large, bright hall where visitors, such as myself, were directed upon arrival. Behind the hall was a dining room and behind that, hidden from sight, was the kitchen. The kitchen pantry took up a significant amount of the ground floor.

There was also a library furnished with imposing English leather armchairs, a bar, and dark, glass-doored bookshelves on both of the long facing walls. There were a lot of books, most of them old.

All of the bedrooms were upstairs. The largest of these was made up of three of the previous bedrooms combined. It had a bathroom designed to the same scale. In the middle of the upper storey was a common room similar to the downstairs hall, though smaller, with double doors leading to a balcony.

The balcony looked out on a view of the sea. From there you could see the entire level, well-tended lawn with its standing rows of junipers, old red and gold maples, on the right the boat shed and dock, where a white, fifteen-metre yacht was moored, and on the left the brown-planked sauna with its terrace and next to it a narrow swimming dock designed for quick dashes into the water.

Standing on the balcony you might make other observations. There were no neighbours. The wind was a constant presence. It whirled over the estate, blowing my hair around, making the woods sigh, and carrying the salty, inviting smell of the sea wherever it went, including indoors. When now and then the wind calmed a little or quieted completely, an extraordinary silence fell, broken only by human sounds.

There were two permanent residents: the cook Enni Salkola, and me. There reigned between us a sort of understanding, a camaraderie. Maybe it was something instinctive, the unspoken thought that we were there to work, unlike those who lived or visited there. There was an *us* and *them*, and that difference placed Enni and me on the same side.

On my second evening there, after spending the whole day working outside in the cool wind, as I was making my way across the dark yard to my apartment, Enni had called after me and invited me into the kitchen for an evening snack. Long, thin slices of fresh rye bread with butter and pickled whitefish, black-label Emmental cheese, and tart apples from the orchard. I was hungry. We talked a bit about our work and nearly as much about the weather, but mostly we ate. And the silence didn't feel bad. When I glanced at Enni while I was eating, she just smiled and asked if I wanted some more. I did.

Standing on the balcony I looked out at the sea. It spread blue and flat before me, as if you could walk on it. I felt the autumn wind on my arms. I checked the floorboards I'd been working on again to make sure they didn't wobble or squeak when you stepped on them. I'd wedged the loose places with small shims and sanded the floor to make everything level. It felt good. I didn't expect anyone to be spending time outside on an autumn weekend, but this small success nevertheless pleased me.

I closed the balcony doors as I went in, swung my toolbag into my right hand, and went downstairs. I walked across the yard to the toolshed first, left my bag there, and then went to the other end of the building, where I was living.

I had my own stairs to the first-floor apartment. I didn't keep the door locked. I didn't see any reason to. I had very few possessions, and the only valuables were valuable only to me. I left my heavy work boots in the doorway, brewed some dark-roasted coffee, and made two sandwiches — Enni's rabbit pâté spread on crusty rye.

I sat by the window and looked at the weak, grey light of the afternoon multiplied in the simple lines and rough, irregular surface of the thick vase I'd placed on the windowsill.

DECEMBER 1993 — JULY 2003

I hadn't noticed it before.

I could feel the social worker's gaze on my back as I walked across the small, quiet apartment to the living-room window.

The home my mother and I shared was going to be sold. I'd been told at various times and in various ways that I couldn't live there alone. I was told that I was only thirteen, that I needed adults around me, to intermediate for me. I didn't argue. I had a different opinion, but I understood that it was useless to resist. After my mother's disappearance it was all inevitable, inexorable, as if a strong, heavy hand had drawn a line between the past and the present, and there was nothing one boy could do about it.

The social worker went into the kitchen. I picked up the vase and I could feel that my mother had once held it in her hand. Maybe she got it from her own mother, a person I knew no more about than I did about anything else. Or maybe she'd found it somewhere and brought it home. In any case, her hands had held it. I went to get a T-shirt from my room to wrap the vase in.

I asked the social worker if I could stay in the apartment one night.

No, that wasn't possible.

I looked the social worker in the eye for a moment. I could tell she felt sorry for me. Everybody did. It didn't bring my mother back or explain what had happened to her.

I went into my room. It was the smallest room in the small apartment, a room of my own. I remembered how my mother had said, Now you have something I never had. I could see tears in her eyes. That happened every now and then. Especially when she talked about her life before me. She said it brought her so much happiness to be able to give this to me. I thought at the time that she was just talking about my room.

I opened the drawers of my scratched, second-hand desk. They were full of stuff. Toys, drawings, scrapbooks, pencils, rubbers, magazines, all kinds of things I'd found and brought home. That heavy hand between past and present had reached here, too. I knew I was no longer the boy who had drawn those pictures, read those magazines, played those games. I was someone else. The old me had gone wherever my mother had gone.

In my mother's room, I sat on the edge of the bed. The room smelled like her and every object looked as if she might come and pick it up at any moment. Her things were already in motion — disappearing from the desk, leaping off the hangers, rising from the floor. I didn't know what to do. The idea that my mother's things would be taken somewhere felt like another disappearance, but at the same time I knew that there was no way I could bring it all with me. I couldn't even bring very much of it.

I looked around.

Two white ribbons as wide as a finger were attached to the top of the decorative black frame of the mirror. I remembered her attaching them there with a twist of wire. I remembered that each of the bows had a story. The first one, the one nearer the centre, at the top of the twist of wire, my mother had tied herself. I recognised it easily. Strong, happy loops. Looking at it, I could see my mother's hands and fingers at work.

I managed to slide the ribbon loose from the wire without untying the knot. The other bow, according to my mother, was from a box of chocolate pastries. Not just any pastries, she said, but homemade pastries for her name day, given to her by an important person at an important moment. It made the bow special. That ribbon had always looked to me as if it didn't match, although it was tied with generous loops like the one my mother had made. It was thicker than hers and there were four loops in it. Looking at it more closely I saw that it wasn't a simple bow knot. It was pulled tight and the knot in the middle was hard as rock. There was someone else's touch in it. I tugged it loose from the mirror frame, closed it in my fist, and walked with both of the bows in my hand back to the windowsill. I dropped the ribbons into the vase and put it under my arm.

I asked the social worker where my mother's things were going.

To a good home, I'm sure, she said.

If it was a good home, could I go there, too?

The social worker tried her best, but her smile wasn't genuine.

That's not quite what I meant, she said.

I didn't say anything. I knew that was *not quite what she meant*. She backed out of the doorway.

My mother wasn't these objects, and she wouldn't be angry that I didn't take them with me. I was only thirteen, but I understood some things. Taking a journey was easier without a lot to carry.

Over the next few years I learned other things, too.

I stopped referring to my mother as missing. Nobody's missing for years and comes back alive. That doesn't happen. My mother was murdered.

When I got out of the army, I rented a tiny studio apartment in the Sörnäinen neighbourhood, and got a position as a carpenter's helper. I liked the job and I liked the carpenter, whose name was Kauko Ranne. He was a head shorter than me, worked from early in the morning until late at night, and encouraged me.

"My work will be done when you can do it better than me," he said. "No one wants to be an assistant; they want to be the boss."

We did subcontracting as well as our own renovations. Ranne demanded a lot and paid well.

One hot, still summer day, I turned on the television. Moments earlier I had been in the shower, rinsing off the dust of the day. I had eaten some beef soup and sat down on the sofa for a cup of coffee.

On a current affairs show they were saying that it had been almost exactly ten years since the country hit the lowest point of the recession of the nineties. They were remembering those who had fallen to the recession and interviewing those who had come through it. One of the survivors was an investor named Henrik Saarinen.

The reporter's jacket flapped in a high wind and his short, thin hair stood up in every direction as he stood with his back to the door that led to the offices of Saarinen's investment firm on Etelä Esplanadi. The reporter outlined Saarinen's portfolio: one-fifth of a media company, almost 5 per cent of a grocery giant, and various holdings in ten different medium-sized Finnish companies.

The programme moved indoors and Saarinen was interviewed in a comfortable conference room that looked more like a gentlemen's salon of a hundred years ago than a modern place of business. On the wall behind Saarinen was a well-known Finnish painting, women on their way to their country cottages at sunset, after a day's work, the sun glowing red and violet on the horizon. The women in the painting looked stricken, worn out, their faces thin and dirty, their clothes ragged. Henrik Saarinen leaned his right elbow on the plump arm of a leather sofa and smiled.

How can a person look friendly and at the same time completely unscrupulous?

That was a question they should have asked Henrik Saarinen, investor. He was nearing sixty and seemed to enjoy being just the age and size that he was. He was a big man, in every way. His grey-blue pinstriped suit, white shirt, and golden yellow necktie seemed stretched tight, although they were undoubtedly custom tailored. His hair was salt and pepper in just that sleek way that speaks of wealth and power. His slightly bloated face either had a hint of sun or was naturally yellowish. His round glasses softened his cool blue eyes, which was no doubt why he wore them. Every time the reporter asked a question, a hint of something like scorn showed in Saarinen's eyes, but since his answers were polite, intelligent, and insightful, he gave the impression of a man who had always been misunderstood, a man who really wanted what was best and did what was best — and what's more, without being asked.

The reporter was taken with his charisma. An interview that had begun combatively was, after four questions, becoming like a visit from a fan. Saarinen told his own version of the recession, of how it was that he had succeeded, had come through splendidly, in fact, and had, according to him, found wise solutions to the problems of Finland's entire economy, just by relying on himself and on that oft-praised invisible hand.

I had always known of Henrik Saarinen's existence. Everybody did. Especially my mother. She had worked for a company that Saarinen owned.

It felt as if I was seeing more than just the interview. The first thing I noticed was his hands — one lying on the arm of the sofa and the other discreetly underscoring his words, eliciting understanding and trust. There was something about his hands. I didn't know what it was, but there was something. His lips, too, which I watched closely, no longer hearing what he was saying. When I didn't listen to the individual words, I could hear the voice, and it sounded as if someone was sitting beside me, turning towards me as he spoke.

I put my cup down on the wood floor and looked at Saarinen's face. It filled my twenty-one-inch television. I tried to understand what it was about the creases in his cheeks and the dark circles under his eyes, obscured for the moment by the almost imperceptible make-up, that I hadn't noticed before, what it was about the shape of his face, the thin, tight lips as they opened and closed that made me feel as if I'd stepped into a dark room that I had to get out of to reach the air and sunlight.

The camera zoomed out and I saw the hands again. The left hand. The one that was sometimes in his lap, sometimes in the air, opening up meanings, inviting you to listen. His fingers rose one by one as he tallied his achievements. I could almost feel his thick fingers, meant for something other than clean, indoor work, touching my hair, the top of my head, my shoulder.

The interview ended.

The reporter continued talking about Henrik Saarinen, who was now shown in a full-length shot, walking and discussing something with three other people in the same art-graced conference room. For a large man of sixty he had a light, springy step. There was no hint of a heavy man's ungainliness or any sign of knee or hip trouble or even the stiffness you would expect in a man of his age.

And when he turned, just as the reporter finished the story with an account of his hobbies (fine art, cuisine, and hunting) — I stepped again into the dark room I'd sensed a moment before. There wasn't anything sharp or quick or in any way remarkable in his movement. It was simply familiar. So familiar that in the darkness I couldn't see anything but his tanned, salt-and-pepper head. The head was talking. The voice came from close by, right next to me, but I still couldn't hear what it was saying.

I turned off the television, sat down, and wrestled my way out of the dark room and back into the sunny summer evening.

I knew something had happened. I'd experienced something unique. I'd been shown something that I already knew, or something I should have known.

SEPTEMBER 2013

I closed the door of the manor house and stood on the veranda. Two plump-breasted crows sat on the roof, utterly still. Against the grey sky they were like those black silhouettes cut from cardboard that people used to buy at amusement parks and hang on the wall to show others something that they already knew — what the person memorialised looked like in profile. Autumn wrapped the land in its groping embrace. I listened to the movement of the gusting wind through the tall spruce trees and the birches that bordered the yard. The air was thin and fresh, with a hint of sap in it, a sweet smell.

I still felt as if I'd stepped into another time, another world. I'd never lived outside Helsinki, though I'd moved all around within the city. First I lived with my mother in Pihlajanmäki, a green, northern suburb of apartment houses, then, after her disappearance, came foster homes in other northern neighbourhoods, and finally a move to the more far-flung Laajasalo, with Reijo and Sinikka. They were an older couple whose children had already left home and they wanted to help the less fortunate. That was the place I learned to call home. For their sake, if for no other reason. When they both died within four years — Sinikka from cancer, Reijo from grief a year later — I felt as if I'd lost my family a second time.

After I finished high school and got out of the army I moved into the city, to the bustle of Sörnäinen. At first I tried to study something, but since I wasn't able to find anything that interested me, I apprenticed to a carpenter. From Sörnäinen I moved to Meilahti, then Alppila. I'd left my second place in Alppila to come here, and as I'd closed the door to my studio apartment for the last time, I had decided that a period of my life was coming to an end, one way or another.

But leaving Helsinki hadn't been the clear, clean break I'd once thought it would be. Love had made my departure difficult and messy. I carried Miia with me, as present as she had been at our last meeting, our last parting.

How could I have done it better? How could I have broken only my own heart?

Expressions of bewilderment and anger took turns on her face.

"I don't understand," she said.

"I find it hard to understand myself . . ."

"That's not what I meant, you conceited, self-centred blockhead. I understand very well what you're doing. You're leaving me. That's perfectly clear. What I don't understand is why you led me to think that I was the most important thing that had ever happened to you."

"You are," I said. "You're the most important pers—"

"Shut up," she said quietly. Her voice was as soft as the day outside the window. The sun was shining warm and butter yellow high over the hill at Torkkelinmäki. In the park outside Miia's window I could see groups of drunks, people walking their dogs, lazing through the summer. They seemed to have a lot of time. "Shut up, Aleksi," she said.

The woman sitting at the table was so lovely that my heart could have broken just at the sight of her. Miia Niemelä, primary school teacher, height 159 centimetres, slightly broad hips, a round face, a laughing mouth, quick with a quip. Not a fashion model or a beauty queen, but so charming that in my eyes she was the most beautiful woman in the city. She was also the best thing that had happened to me in twenty years. But I had my past and I had my future, and one was just as hard to explain as the other.

I simply didn't know how to tell her how it feels to lose your mother at the age of thirteen. I didn't know how to describe how it felt to carry something like that with you for twenty years, the kinds of thoughts it makes you think, the way it affects everything. And I couldn't tell her what I was planning to do about it. I couldn't tell her about signing on at Kalmela Manor, and I couldn't tell her about Henrik Saarinen. I didn't know how.

"Is this just what you do?" Miia asked. Her brown eyes shone, her bare, delicate shoulders glowed tan on either side of her sleeveless shirt. "You tell women they're important when they aren't? I can't believe I've been so naive. I've seen everything. I'm thirty-two years old. This isn't my first time around the block. I can't believe it but somehow, I don't know why, I trusted you."

I had meant everything I'd said — that she was the best thing that had ever happened to me, the first person who ever made me believe in myself and believe in someone else, believe that life with a woman could be more than just a fight, more than just a combination of sex and power games, that even I had a chance at something better.

"I've been honest with you," I said, because I didn't know what else to say.

"Honest?" she said, looking at me. "What do you know about honesty?"

Quite a lot, I thought. At least I knew that the greatest honesty doesn't always mean revealing your every darkest thought.

"Miia . . ."

"Forget it. I saw a different kind of man in you. A different kind of person. That's all."

I wanted to say that what she saw was true. That I was that kind of man. That I could be.

Miia's apartment was a studio — one bright, high-ceilinged room and a microscopic bathroom. There was little furniture but all of it was well-chosen and beautiful. A dark brown antique peasant cabinet stood solid beside me as I tried to find a place to put my feet. I couldn't find one. I leaned against the wall. Finding the right words was just as difficult. I'd never been in this situation before. How could I have been? To love and leave at the same time? My mother was the only person I'd ever loved, and she was taken away from me. After that I'd done nothing but lust, hate, and fight. And leave. I didn't know what to do. Didn't know how to do it.

"Get it over with. Tell me what all this is about. Let me know what to be angry about. Tell me you have another woman, or you've realised you like men, or you're a secret agent — anything."

"There's nothing to tell. No other woman, nothing."

"How long have we been going out?"

"Six months and eleven days," I said.

Miia looked at me, her eyes filled with such a searching fury that it spilled out of the corners of her eyes and down her sun-browned cheeks, cheeks that I loved to smell and touch.

"Why do you say it like that," she said quietly.

"Like what?"

"You can tell me down to the day how long we've been together, but you're breaking up with me. Do you realise how crazy that sounds? How crazy it makes me feel?"

"I'm sorry."

"Then you say you're sorry. I'm sorry, Miia, you're the best thing ever, but I have to leave. Jesus."

The day was positively glowing outside, the sky blue from one end to the other, smooth as the cover of a book. Young men were lying in the park with their shirts off. The thought of cool grass on my back felt enticing, and utterly foreign.

"Why do you have to do this," Miia suddenly asked, wiping her eyes with the back of her hand. I could see a tear clinging to her cheek. I was surprised by her question. Surprised that I'd said something that gave her that idea.

"Well, I . . ."

I couldn't tell her that I *had* to move to Kalmela within the next two weeks, that I *had* to do it because I planned to find out what Henrik Saarinen had done to my mother, that I *had* to because if I didn't, I'd never stop thinking about it.

"What?"

"I just have to."

"If it's not another woman and it's not that you're some weirdo and you're not in the service of a foreign power, then it must be about you. And I thought I'd got to know you. I realise now that the only you I've got to know is how you are now, today. Do you understand what I'm talking about?"

Of course I did. I had purposely avoided, dodged and ducked any discussion of my past, especially my family. In other words, my mother. The official version — the one I'd told Miia — was that my mother was dead. That was true. And what I'd told her about my father was also true, of course — that I didn't really know anything about him.

"But your face doesn't lie," Miia said.

I loved her for this, too. Her ability to see what I really was, who I was.

"Miia," I said.

She didn't look at me.

"Leave."

And that had been it — the last word that Miia had ever spoken to me.

I went down the stairs and headed for the sauna. I'd been given the use of the all-terrain quad bike and trailer, too, but I'd only needed it one time. If I didn't have anything heavy to carry, like my tools or building supplies, I preferred to walk. I always had. Walking was best in every way. You never got anywhere too soon. Your thoughts straightened out; things fell into proportion. The restlessness left your body, the dead ends left your mind. You got where you were going step by step, both in the world and inside yourself.

The narrow gravel path wound around the manor house and sloped down to the left side of the lawn. From there it continued almost straight down to the beach. On the shore you turned left, walked a couple of dozen steps, and came to what they called the main sauna. The log building covered in board cladding was built long before present building codes and stood as close to the water as was physically possible. If you'd wanted it any closer you would have had to build it in the Venetian style. It did, in fact, have pilings in the water. A terrace for small parties was built over the sea at the front of the building. The sauna was the size of a small, one-storey house, pale yellow like the manor, with a black roof and a chimney as big as a factory's.

I inspected the washrooms, both dressing rooms, and the large hearth room. The high windows looked out over the water. The sea and sky were full of colours and hypnotic movement. Pale rifts moved through the mass of clouds, flowing across the sky like rivers, meandering, dotted with rapids. The sea looked almost black one moment, and shone an unreal blue the next. It changed its spots like a living creature, moving first left, then right.

I went over the terrace as carefully as I had the sauna house.

This was the main part of my job. Making sure that the place was kept in good condition, making necessary repairs. For larger jobs I paid someone who specialised in whatever needed to be done, and the estate had a cleaning service. All that was left that I had time for, I took care of myself, and I was happy to do it. I needed more time, and I could have it if I did my job well.

The water lapped against the stones on the shore as I walked the short way from the terrace to the boat dock. There were two boats tied to it.

The larger one was white and surprisingly tall, all of its windows dark. On the other side of the dock was an aluminium skiff with a large outboard motor. I walked past it to the end of the dock. When I moved the couple of dozen metres away from the shore the wind greeted me with a stiff slap.

There was a swimmer's ladder leading up from the cold water. The dock swayed. I turned back towards the shore, my back to the open sea. The manor stood on its hill under the sky like something in a picture. I let my gaze slide along the shoreline metre by metre. A broken, rocky shore, and beyond that dense forest.

Soon I saw movement among the maple trees and recognised her hair. I stood at the tip of the dock, letting the wind push against my back. The quad bike pulled up at the other end; the motor stopped. I could hear steps on the dock and feel them through the soles of my feet.

Amanda Saarinen had changed clothes. She'd returned from wherever it was she had gone, and she'd done it quickly. She was wearing coveralls and carrying a rod and reel and a tackle box. I didn't know which was more out of place, Amanda in her fishing outfit or me, a stranger here. She must have noticed my expression, because she said, "Don't look so surprised. I fish. Do you?"

"No," I said quietly, trying to get my mind around the idea of a fishing heiress.

"Do you hunt?"

"No," I said again, and imagined Amanda with a rifle in her hand. The image it conjured up seemed surprisingly natural.

"Why not?"

"I've never felt the need."

"Have you ever tried it?"

"No."

Where would I have bagged an elk or angled for trout? In Sörnäinen? I didn't tell Amanda that not everyone is born with a five-hundred-euro fishing rod in his hand and his own waterfront property, or a thousand-euro suede boot to put on the Range Rover's accelerator.

Her eyes flashed. Her hair was so thick that the wind couldn't lift it all at once.

"It's getting windy, but tomorrow it should be sunny," she said, more to herself than to me.

"I hope so."

We stood on the dock a couple of metres apart. Amanda was a slim, delicate woman. Her nose was sharp, her chin slightly wide. There were faint lines around her eyes. She looked past me, out to sea. I was pondering how to get away as quickly and politely as possible when she said, "Will you help me?"

She pointed at the boat. I stood next to her, leaned over, took hold of the rope and pulled. When the bow was almost touching the dock she stepped into the boat with her rod and tackle box, in one smooth, unbroken motion. Her soft, silent movements made an impression, whether I wanted them to or not. There were a lot of things about Amanda that impressed me. Like the way she effortlessly maintained her balance. She put down the box and rod, glanced at the motor, and put a key in the ignition. I stood staring at her.

"When it's your own boat, you know where everything is," she said.

"That's what I was thinking."

"I forgot something. Could you pull the boat in?"

She stepped onto the dock with the same smooth combination of movements and started digging in her pockets.

"I wonder if it's in there," she said, nodding towards the larger, white boat.

"What do you need?"

"A knife. It's not in my box for some reason."

"You need it for fishing?"

"On the sea . . . You need all kinds of things on the sea."

"There's a basic set of tools in the quad bike. There's probably a knife in there."

I walked to the four-wheeler and took the toolbox out of the trailer. There was a small collection of tools inside, including a yellow-handled knife in a black plastic sheath. I carried it to Amanda, who was watching the water again.

"Thanks."

"No problem. Remember to return it."

I didn't mean it as a joke, but a little smile came to Amanda's lips as she slipped the knife into the breast pocket of her coveralls.

"What about a life jacket?" I asked.

"Are you worried?"

I looked her in the eye. I thought about why I was here, what was most important. I didn't want to think about Amanda, her life, or her seafaring habits. I'd already let the conversation go too far.

"It probably won't turn stormy," I said. "Just a bit of wind."

Amanda didn't say anything. She looked at the open water again for a moment, tugged on the zipper of her coveralls, although they were already zipped up, and jumped into the boat. I took a deep breath of the salty air and thought that this strange encounter, the second one today, was over. Just then she turned. There was a break in the clouds, the sun's rays pierced the world, a gust of wind took hold of her hair and the strong light reflected in her eyes in a way that seemed to dazzle me more than it did her.

She started the motor and loosened the rope. The boat moved away from the dock, backed up, and swung out towards the empty crest of the sea as the sun disappeared behind the clouds again.

AUGUST 1993

Mum . . .

The room is dark as if it, too, had covered itself in a blanket. I hear my mother breathing at the end of the sofa. The living room is small and long, the sofa against the wall facing the kitchen.

Don't turn the light on, she says.

Why? I ask.

She doesn't answer.

I know the way to the sofa. First my bare feet find the edge of the shag rug. Two or three careful soft steps over the carpet, then my shins touch the thick edge of the table, from there my left hand follows the table to the sofa and I make a little turn and sit down. My mother's sitting at the other end.

You should be asleep, she says.

I woke up.

I can see that.

Is it late?

It's very late. Too late.

Was the party nice?

Yes.

Then why are you sitting in the dark?

Because the party was so nice.

I don't understand what she means. I can smell that she's been drinking alcohol.

Why don't you want the lights on? I ask.

I want to sit and think for a minute. Undisturbed.

Are you tired?

I'm sure I am, a little.

Shouldn't you go to sleep, then?

I should. And you especially should, my little sweetheart.

I'm not little any more.

But you're still a sweetheart.

We sit quietly for a moment. The building changes at night into a living creature. It breathes, drinks, gurgles, pees, clatters, moves through the night as if through outer space, flying, weightless.

What was so nice about the party? I ask.

People, she says. A person.

A certain person?

Yes.

What kind of person?

A nice person.

What's this nice person like?

You ask an awful lot of questions. You should stop asking and start sleeping.

I'm awake.

The kind of nice person I haven't met in a long time.

Who is it?

Let's talk about it some other time.

What's nice about him?

She doesn't say anything.

Don't you plan to go to sleep at all?

In a minute.

Should I bring you a blanket?

No. I'm going to sit for a while, then I'll go to bed.

Promise?

I promise.

I have a match tomorrow.

I know.

Are you going to come and watch it?

Of course.

But you'll be tired if you stay up.

This is the kind of staying up that doesn't make you tired.

How can you stay up and not be tired?

You can when you're happy.

I thought you were happy before you went to the party.

I was. And now I'm even happier.

Oh. Because of this nice person?

You guessed it, Sherlock. I love you. Now go to bed.

I will if you will.

All right.

She gets up from the sofa, and so do I.

I go to my bed and get under the blanket. Before I fall asleep I hear her in the bathroom. She's humming. Almost silently. But in the quiet, in the building drifting weightless through the night, I recognise the song.

Don't you forget about me.

SEPTEMBER 2013

The rain started as I was warming the sauna. At first it fell from the sky in large drops, as if someone were tossing them onto the earth one at a time. I'd filled the firebox with thin sticks of birch, piling them in crossed rows with pieces of newspaper in between, and managed to light it with one match. The firebox hummed with hungry flames as I closed the steam-room door behind me.

From the sauna porch I could see heavy drops falling on the water like little stones. Their number quickly grew and soon the water was like the surface of the moon, rough and black as space.

If there was one thing I liked about this place it was the sauna. I had permission to warm it up even when the owner wasn't there. The day before I'd done just that. The steam of the wood-heated sauna was sweet and leisurely, falling over my back like a hot, soothing cloak. I went straight from the sauna into the sea and swam a little circuit in the freezing water. After that I'd sat on the terrace breathing peacefully, languid, and forgotten for a moment who I was, why I'd come here.

There was still just one boat at the dock, Amanda Saarinen's boat was nowhere to be seen. The wind grew stronger. The drops were smaller and angrier. There were more of them, falling thick. At first only a few waves had tufts of foam on them, then more and more. The wind was growing colder and fiercer.

I listened for a motor but all I could hear was the sea, in thousands of surging waves, and a wind that pushed everything before it — the rain, the sauna house, the trees on the shore. What did it matter to me if somebody wanted to defy the sea and rain and wind, the whole world?

Visibility was abysmal. I turned on the lights that hung from the posts around the sauna terrace. They were just party lights, of course, but even so, you might be able to get your bearings from them, provided you could get them in view. I looked at the waves and thought about the aluminium boat floating on them. The wind was so strong now that I had to shift my stance to get a firmer footing. The cold rain froze my face and hands.

I thought that if the waves close to shore were this high, heavy whitecaps crashing together, then the situation out on the water must be much worse. How far off were the good fishing spots? It wasn't my concern, of course. Boats in trouble could call the coast guard. Boats in trouble had to do that themselves. But what if someone was in trouble and didn't have a phone with her?

Before I realised what I was doing I had walked to the dock, and all the way to the end. I was wet through.

I took a couple of steps to the left, then the right. I kept my eyes on the water. I tried to shove my hands in my pockets to warm them, but my trousers were so cold and pasted to my legs that it did no good. The waves were growing before my eyes. The wind had changed to a steady gale. It felt like standing in a wind tunnel. The rain struck my face with so much force that my skin stung. I was shaking with cold. I wiped my eyes and squinted out at the dark water.

I heard the sound of an outboard motor. First in bursts, like a chainsaw or lawnmower that won't start. Then I saw a clear, lone little light. I stood for a moment longer on the dock to assure myself of what I saw and heard. The sound grew louder, although it still disappeared completely at intervals. The light disappeared, too, intermittently, but it always came back again. I thought of the boat on the high waves, rising atop one and sinking between them again.

As the sound of the motor became clearer and the light shone more and more often and stayed in view for longer stretches of time, I started to feel stupid. As if I'd been caught at something. But what?

The aluminium boat tossed like a feather on the towering waves. At times it was at the crest of a wave and almost perpendicular to the dock, but it maintained its direction. A few frozen minutes passed. Then I heard Amanda's voice through the sound of the motor, the waves, and the wind. She was asking for help mooring.

The boat's bright light lit up the dark like a tenacious little sun. Amanda stood up, got the rear rope tied to the buoy, took hold of the rudder and, with the rope in one hand, steered and opened the throttle to bring the boat closer to the dock, then took a couple of steps towards the bow, threw me the bow rope, stepped back and, once she'd seen that the boat was close enough, killed the engine, tied her own rope off, and went forward again. Without speaking, she threw me another bow line. I tied it off, too. The cold had numbed my fingers. It felt as if I was watching someone else's hands tie the knots.

I reached out to help her ashore. I couldn't see her face. Her hand was small in mine and she made her way off the boat as nimbly as she had boarded it.

I turned almost immediately and we walked to the sauna. Amanda walked beside me. She still hadn't spoken. She had a bucket in one hand and in it were some perch with their bellies sliced open. The essence of the past hour seemed to be concentrated in those open bodies — the denial of what I knew was going to happen, the inevitability of it, the bad feeling I had about where all this was leading to.

A thought came to me from somewhere back in history class about priestesses in ancient Greece or Rome predicting the future from the entrails of fish, then I drifted back to this moment, the paleness of Amanda's face and the knowledge of how handy she was with a knife, and the image of an heiress who hunted and fished felt logical now, completely mundane.

We stopped on the sauna porch. We were sheltered from the rain, but not the wind.

In the light on the porch I saw her face. Her cheekbones stood out. Her skin looked thin, transparent.

"Thanks for the help," she said, and turned to look at me. Her eyes, framed by her damp black hair and her bone-white face in the artificial light, were like wet, blue-grey pearls.

Water streamed onto the floor of the terrace. She looked into my eyes again.

"Excellent."

"What is?"

"This," she said, lifting up her bucket to show me the three large perch, their gutted bellies like broad, cold smiles. "I'll make us some supper. We'll eat in half an hour."

JULY 2003

The officer's name was Ketomaa. He had been the principal investigator of my mother's case in the Helsinki Police violent crimes unit. He was the one with the shiny forehead, the man who told me in a patient voice that my mother was missing. Now, eight years later, he listened to my story without speaking, and when I'd finished, asked, "On television?"

"Yes. The other night. Some current events show where they interviewed people about the recession at the beginning of the nineties."

"Henrik Saarinen?"

"Yes."

Ketomaa leaned back in the metal café chair. The shore of Kaivopuisto was humming with people in the summer heat — tourists, Helsinki locals, people of all ages, sizes, and shapes. We'd succeeded in finding a quiet table at the edge of the café terrace. Ketomaa had sunglasses perched on his nose, the kind that had been out of fashion for ten or fifteen years.

"They transferred the case to the central police years ago," he said.

"This is easy to check. Just find out where Henrik Saarinen was on the ninth of October, 1993. The police must have ways of doing that."

Ketomaa didn't answer. His face was turned toward Suomenlinna Island. The sun burned almost white above us, at its highest point of the year. The heat felt like a suit of clothes you couldn't take off.

Ketomaa tasted his lemon soda. He wiped his mouth with the back of his hand.

"How are things with you?" he said.

"What do you mean?"

"Your life. Have you finished school? Found work?"

"University student. Carpenter."

"Good. I'm glad."

Ketomaa was a tall, thin man. His forehead shone as brightly as ever. He had his right leg thrown over his left, one foot reaching down like a giraffe bending to drink. He seemed to think for a moment, then adjusted his sunglasses.

"I'm sorry," he said at last. "I was given the case and I did my best, but we don't have anything. We were in the dark from beginning to end."

"That's why I'm telling you this," I said.

He let the comment pass. He did it deftly, as if my words were evaporating in the heat.

"One minute your mother was at work, working overtime with two other people, and the next minute she wasn't. Her coat was left on the back of her chair, her bag was on her desk, with her wallet in it, next to a stack of receipts and a cup of coffee with milk and sugar. Her co-workers thought she'd gone to the toilet.

Then an hour passed and they started to wonder where she was. They looked for her. The ground-floor door was unlocked. Maybe it just happened to be unlocked, or maybe it was left that way on purpose. Your mother doesn't smoke, so she had no need to go out there. And since she doesn't smoke, we couldn't check cigarette butts to see if she was the one who'd opened the door. Another hour went by, then another. In the morning the police arrived. I arrived."

Ketomaa loosened his tie. His armpits were wet through.

"There were no clues on her phone. Later — too late — we thought of looking around the building — tyre tracks, things like that. It had rained, of course. It was October. We got nothing from the surveillance cameras. We searched for cars based on witnesses' statements. Nothing. We went through every possibility — public transport, airports, everything. We checked her bank account, combed through your apartment."

He stopped speaking and took a drink.

"I know all that," I said.

"I know you know."

"So?"

"Without a body, we have nothing."

"Can't we have a suspect first? A murder suspect?"

"For that there has to be a murder. There isn't one. There's no basis for suspecting anyone of anything."

Seagulls screeched. A crack appeared in Ketomaa's concrete exterior. His voice grew thin.

"I can only imagine how you must feel. I feel bad. I can't even fathom what your feelings are. I'm sure all kinds of things come into your mind, hunches based on one thing or another."

"My mother said she'd met someone."

"I know. We've had this conversation."

"Why would I have that kind of feeling about Saarinen if he had nothing to do with it? Why was his voice familiar to me?"

Ketomaa turned away and looked out at the islands. I looked at the back of his head. His earlobe was nearly transparent against the sea and sky. He adjusted his sunglasses and turned back towards me.

"This is just between us. Of course we knew who owned the business. And of course we went through everything connected with the job, the workplace, the business, and its owner. And we did find something, but it didn't have anything to do with your mother or her disappearance."

"What did you find?"

"Nothing significant. And I can't tell you about it. But it had nothing at all to do with your mother. It had to do with Henrik Saarinen. We were going to question him, but he was in Stockholm at the time. So that was that."

"Stockholm?"

"Yes."

"A person can get here from Stockholm in an hour . . ."

Ketomaa dropped his right leg off his left and turned in his chair so nimbly that I forgot his height, and his age — nearing sixty.

"A person can get here from Stockholm in an hour and kidnap a woman and hide her body without a trace, particularly if he's the boss and everyone in the place recognises him. And in another hour he can be back in Stockholm. Because he never actually left. Some things just are what they are and there's nothing we can do to change them. Saarinen isn't connected to this case."

His sunglasses were pointed directly at me. I assumed that the pale grey eyes behind their dark brown lenses were staring me straight in the eye.

"You sound certain," I said.

Ketomaa opened his mouth but didn't say anything. He turned his profile to me again and leaned back in his chair. We sat for a moment in silence. A champagne cork popped a couple of tables away, a happy hurrah went up, the bottle clinked against the rims of the glasses.

"We did what we could," he said.

"Are you sure?" I asked.

"It was ten years ago."

"What kind of answer is that?"

He slid his soda bottle a centimetre forward, a centimetre back.

"When a case is left unsolved, everyone feels uncertain. What should we have done differently? What did we miss? Who's to blame? Where's the weak link?"

He loosened his fingers from the bottle, laid his hand on the table.

"I understand you better than you think I do. You were thirteen. I remember you. That first night. It felt unfair. I understand that it still troubles you."

"Not any more. I know who did it."

Ketomaa took off his sunglasses and turned to face me. The whites of his grey eyes were threaded with red.

"I don't have children of my own. There was a time when I thought that by doing this kind of work I could help somebody have a better life. Sort of lead them in the right way. Give something. That's what I thought that day. Did I succeed? Maybe not. Time will tell."

He looked at the sea, squinting.

"I hope you learn how to let go. No matter what happens, no matter how tragic it might be, you have to keep moving forward. I once heard someone say that life doesn't let you stand still. You can't just lie there when you're under fire. If you don't force yourself to move forward you'll start sliding backwards."

I noticed that I hadn't touched my coffee. I didn't know why I'd ordered it in this furnace. There was a splotch of fat on the surface that looked like an accident. Ketomaa continued.

"You only have one life. You're young and you have all kinds of possibilities. Don't ruin it by starting to see personal messages everywhere you look, or hear the television talking directly to you. I see people like that every day on the job. They don't fare well. Ever. Obsessions don't have happy endings."

He leaned his elbows on his knees, looked at me again, and swung his unfashionable sunglasses in his hand. I didn't say anything. Ketomaa sighed and put the glasses back on. We watched in silence as a boat slipped slowly past with its sails lowered.

SEPTEMBER 2013

The cutlery clinked against the white plates and the rustle of my napkin was like the roar of a waterfall as I lifted it to wipe my mouth. I had tried to locate Enni in the kitchen or its vicinity but I didn't hear her bustling activity or the usual groan she emitted when getting up, bending over, or otherwise exerting herself. Maybe she'd surrendered the kitchen as a favour to Amanda and walked the short distance to her apartment, which was in the restored barn.

Although I felt uncomfortable and was trying my best to be on my guard, I had to admit that the food was good. The perch fillets were lightly breaded, seasoned with garlic, and fried in butter, the mashed potatoes were creamy and the roasted beetroot and carrots were crisp on the outside and soft in the middle. I praised the meal. Amanda glanced at me.

"Enni is a master," she said. "Still no wine for you?"

"No, thanks," I said.

"None at all? Ever?"

"Not today."

She looked at me for a moment and poured some white wine for herself. I didn't want to explain why I wasn't drinking. One glass always led to another, and a third, and a tenth, and eventually to decisions and deeds that I later regretted.

I finished the last bite, set my knife and fork on the edge of my plate, wiped my mouth and tucked the dark green paper napkin under the edge of my plate. I looked up and my eyes once again met Amanda's.

"If you're wondering whether I offer dinner to all the maintenance men, the answer is no," she said. "This is the first time. It's rare that I'm surprised by a storm. I wanted to chat with you."

I didn't say anything. Amanda tasted her wine before speaking again.

"You see that? If you were anyone else you would have asked me why I want to chat with you, what about. But you're not asking. You go with the flow, take whatever comes. You're quiet and just — I don't know — waiting, I suppose. That's what you're doing. Waiting. There's nothing wrong with that. In fact I wish I could do the same. Wish I could have done the same."

"When?" I asked.

Amanda smiled. Or that's how I interpreted the flash of her white teeth, anyway.

"You're sharp. You always steer the conversation to something other than yourself."

I leaned back in my chair as far as I could. I thought it was still a little too early to say good night. And after the relaxing sauna and dinner, I thought, let things flow where they will, let the conversation carry you along. But be careful.

"There must be some reason for your guardedness," Amanda said. "You're not afraid of me, are you? I'm sure there's no need to be. There's no one else in the house. I'm twenty centimetres shorter than you, and thirty kilos lighter. I'm the one who ought to be wary. I don't know you. The closest neighbour besides Enni is almost a kilometre away. I just thought we might have something in common."

She leaned her elbows on the table. I noticed how little she'd eaten. She'd hardly touched her dinner. My own plate was nearly licked clean. I tried to interpret the expression on her face, keeping well in mind who she was, and whose daughter.

"I don't know what that would be," I said.

"Can't you think of anything?"

I didn't answer.

"I'm not trying to hit on you, by the way," she said. "I can make conversation, can't I? Are you married?"

"No."

"Girlfriend?"

I thought about Miia. I shook my head.

"Not even a girlfriend."

She picked up her wineglass and looked over it at me. The thoughts that entered my mind as I took in her dark eyes, framed by make-up, her full, wet lips, her slender hands and arms and ample breasts, weren't the kind I particularly needed. I reminded myself again why I'd come to Kalmela, why I was sitting there like a good boy, why it was generally a good idea to keep my distance and give her a certain impression: I planned to catch the father of the woman across from me for what he had done twenty years ago, I planned to find out how he had murdered my mother. If this required me to play my part flawlessly, I would.

"What about you?" I asked.

Amanda smiled. "What about me? I'm a rich man's daughter. That tells you something, doesn't it? I was married once, and engaged twice, and now I'm by myself. I studied finance and used to work in a brokerage firm. Now I'm focused on other things."

"What does it tell you? Being a rich man's daughter?"

She leaned forward again. Her low collar opened a little further.

"That people who try to get close to me aren't necessarily doing it for my sake. My ex-husband's a good example. Ilari. His name alone should have been a warning to me. Think about it. Ilari. What does that sound like?"

It sounded to me like a man's name.

"Ilari was perfect. From good stock, a fine, well-to-do family. My mother and father were so happy. I'm sure Ilari's parents were, too. No one asked whether I was happy. Not even Ilari. Least of all him. But what of it? I didn't know anything about what Ilari was thinking anyway. Would you like some wine?"

"No thank you. Still none for me."

She looked into her glass. She drank, ran her tongue over her upper lip, licking a drop of wine into her mouth. Then she rubbed her nose.

"It was a horrible life," she said.

A rich man's daughter who made a wealthy marriage, I thought. It must have been a horrible, hard life.

"I just did what I was expected to do," she said, "because I wanted to be liked. Isn't that the real reason people do things? To be loved?"

Maybe she did have some cracks in her shell, like everyone else. Little fissures that were hidden by her appearance and her lifestyle and her black SUV, and fishing and hunting and silicone breasts and everything else. I couldn't see the cracks, but that didn't mean they weren't there.

"You mentioned your mother," I said.

Amanda lifted her elbows off the table.

"What about her?"

"She must not be still . . ."

"The old witch lives in Spain. She's lived there most of my life, for nineteen years. And I haven't really seen her since they divorced years before that and I ended up living mostly with my father, which is unusual, of course. But I suppose my life is unique in lots of ways."

My mother disappeared twenty years ago, I thought, and a year later Henrik Saarinen's wife moved to Spain. The two things might be connected, or they might not.

"Why did your mother move there?" I asked.

Amanda's expression changed. She looked serious, her head tilted slightly to the right. She looked exceptionally beautiful.

"How the fuck should I know?" she said quietly. "Maybe she likes sunshine more than sleet. Why ask me that?"

"Just wondering," I said, knowing that I needed to back off. "I can make conversation, can't I?"

"Can you?" Amanda smiled, her face lighting up as instantaneously as it had turned serious a moment before. "That's a question you ought to ask yourself. I don't talk to her. There's nothing to talk about."

"Right," I said, trying to think of another subject, but Amanda already had.

"Where do you come from? I've told you everything. Now it's your turn."

"I think I told you at breakfast," I said, "I'm a carpenter by trade —"

"I mean the part of your life that's interesting. Ex-wives? Children? Skeletons in the closet?"

Skeletons in the closet? Just one. My mother. Who was murdered by your father.

"I guess not," I said. "No ex-wives, no children, nothing. I'm a rather dull person. An ordinary guy in every way. Very even-keel in the relationship department."

That last sentence wasn't true. My life had been one long storm before Miia. Miia, who I'd left to come here, who I missed terribly, passionately. Physically, too, which was probably the reason that my eyes kept straying to Amanda's skin and lips and striking eyes. It was a good thing I wasn't drinking.

"What else," she asked, pouring yet another glass of wine.

"I live in Helsinki. I've lived there all my life."

"What part?"

"Most recently in Alppila."

58

"It occurs to me that we're roughly the same age and Helsinki is, in a way, a small town."

She looked at me as she took a drink. I remembered something I'd read long ago — by F. Scott Fitzgerald, one of my mother's favourite authors — that the rich are different from you and me. I could see it in Amanda. The way she picked up her glass, drank, talked, sat in a chair. It lacked the weight that ordinary people have on their shoulders. As she looked at me I knew that she didn't understand anything about ordinary life. She took a drink of her wine and continued.

"Are you sure we've never met at all, even in passing?"

"I would remember you," I said, and understood even without Amanda's smile what I'd said.

"I'll take that as a compliment," she said, and again I felt caught out. "I just have that feeling. Like we have some connection."

I shook my head. I felt something tearing me up inside.

"I don't think so. I don't think we've ever run into each other, I mean."

I had to get out of there.

"I ought to thank you for the dinner now."

"Already?"

"It's pretty late, and I have to start work at seven."

"Whatever you say."

She got up from her chair, and I did the same. Before I'd even pushed my chair in Amanda had come around the table and stood in front of me. She was standing between me and the door. She came closer, put her hands on my arms, and kissed me on the cheek. The kiss was just too long.

"Thanks for the company."

I looked into her shining eyes, smelled her soft perfume and the wine on her breath, saw her pale skin and moist lips in the candlelight, and knew that if I had even a drop of alcohol or stayed even a minute longer, something would happen that I couldn't afford.

"Thanks for dinner. It was all very good. The food, and especially the company."

She loosened her grip on my arms and took a step backwards. She smiled. It wasn't a happy smile; there was something else in it.

"Good night, then."

"Good night, Amanda."

I stepped past her and realised that at any other time I would have turned at that moment, stood in front of her and waited for her to tilt her head ever so slightly back, answered with a careful, polite kiss, and depending on her response, kept going, or backed off, having had a taste of those perfect lips.

I walked through the half-darkened hall to the foyer and opened the front door.

The rain had stopped and the wind was almost totally calm. The air was still and moist, the night standing motionless, as if it were waiting for something.

SEPTEMBER 2013

"Henrik is coming today."

Enni's voice was a mixture of soldierly respect and motherly tenderness. She was standing in front of the window looking out, as if to get a glimpse of the lion soon to arrive. I knew that there was nothing to see. Amanda's black Range Rover had disappeared. I thought it unlikely that she had been in any condition to drive when she left. But Enni didn't care about Amanda. She was waiting for Henrik Saarinen's long, grey, chauffeured Mercedes-Benz.

Outside was a wistful, calm autumn day filled with golden sunlight. There wasn't a trace of the night-time storm and winds as the light slanted into the room tinged with a soft yellow. It made Enni's fiftyish face older, rounder. Her hair, worn twisted into a bun, had streaks of grey here and there that lit up brighter the closer she leaned toward the window.

I'd listened before coming into the kitchen to be sure it was empty. I'd found what I needed to make a sandwich, brewed a large cup of black coffee, and sat down at the table to eat, when Enni gave me a fright by appearing out of nowhere.

I couldn't tell where she'd come from. I was sure that I knew the house now, knew what it sounded like when someone was there, how the sounds carried from room to room. But there she was next to me as I took a bite of oat bread wet with pickle, behaving as if it was completely normal that I should walk right in and sit down in her domain, the inner sanctum, although I'd never done it before.

I thought of what I knew about Enni. Not much; our conversations had been short and practical, information about our work and the weather and general manor business.

"How long have you been working here?" I asked.

Enni stayed by the window facing the yard, but her eyes glanced quickly at me before returning to the gravel drive where the king would ride to his castle.

"Why do you ask?"

"I was just wondering."

"Why were you wondering that?"

I looked at her. She seemed stiff, almost frozen in position. Her fingers were stretched straight where they hung by her side.

"It just occurred to me. You must know what the owner likes."

She glanced at the clock on the wall.

"Food-wise," I added.

"Yes, I do," Enni said, stepping away from the window towards the countertops, the stove, her territory. She seemed to relax. She looked me in the eye in her familiar, distantly polite way. "Of course I do. I've been here almost exactly twenty years."

"More or less than twenty years?"

I tried my best to sound less interested in this than I was.

"I came here in 1993. I started in November to give me time to get used to the place before taking care of the arrangements for my first Christmas."

My mother disappeared in October 1993. A month later Enni started picking out the ham for Henrik Saarinen's Christmas dinner.

"How did it go, the first Christmas?"

"It went well. I was already . . ." Her eyes sought the window again. "I mean everything was more difficult in the beginning. Before I'd settled in and got to know . . . Things become familiar. And you learn who likes what. I'm sure it's the same in your work."

I'm sure it is.

"Henrik Saarinen was still married then?"

"Yes. Or rather . . . Helena was already mostly in Spain, but officially they were still married."

"So he was mostly alone here?"

Enni tilted her head as if she wanted to get a look at me from a different angle. Perhaps to see something that wasn't visible before. I was still sitting at the table with a half-eaten sandwich on my plate and a mug of coffee in front of me.

"I guess so," she said. "I never thought about it."

"Were there other people working here then?"

She swung her hand up to her waist.

"Twenty years ago? Why would you want to know that? After all you weren't more than . . ."

"Thirteen," I said.

"There were more permanent staff. There are just two of us now."

"Here in the house?"

"No," Enni said. "Taking care of the garden and maintenance. It was just me in the house."

There was pride in her voice as she said this.

"It's a big house for one man," I said.

"That depends how you look at it. A big man should have a big house. That's my opinion."

"What about Amanda? She was just little then. Not even a teenager. Was she here alone?"

I looked at Enni and ate my sandwich. There was a smile on her face now. A knowing, almost sly smile.

"Forget Amanda," she said.

I swallowed. That wasn't what I had meant.

"I knew it," Enni said, not waiting for my response. "I told Elias that this would happen when he said that the new caretaker was about thirty. I thought, that's too young. Someone that age can still get ideas in his head. Not know his place, not understand how things work."

The coffee had gone cold. I drank it anyway. I waited for Enni to continue, but she turned away and didn't say anything more. She started working, bending over the lower cupboards, putting a mixing bowl on the counter, opening the food cupboards, seemingly absorbed in searching for something.

"When is he coming?" I asked.

She didn't look at me when she answered. Around dusk. She didn't know exactly when. She cut pats of butter as big as slices of cake into the mixing bowl.

"He'll want a sauna in the evening, of course," she said, still not looking at me. "And he'll want to see you. All of us. It's customary."

"Should we all stand in a row like in British movies? Those films about the life of the nobility?"

"I told Elias you were too young," Enni said. She seemed to be smiling to herself, I thought I could hear it in her voice. "Much too young."

AUGUST 2003

Tanja Metsäpuro disappeared in August of 2003.

I followed the case in the news and I could see from the start that it wasn't an ordinary one, not some drunken person who leaves a bar and is found in the nearest river with no indication of a crime. The same feeling of sure recognition, of instinctive knowledge that I'd had sitting in front of the television two years earlier shot through me.

Tanja Metsäpuro was a 31-year-old hairdresser and single mother of two daughters who had hired a babysitter on a Saturday night and was enjoying a rare evening out in a Vantaa nightclub with a group of friends.

A little after midnight she got up from the table, and never returned. Her friends noticed this at four a.m., when the lights flashed for last orders. None of them had paid any attention earlier, for obvious reasons. They were all in a party mood and concentrating on their own enjoyment. There was only one member of the group who said she had wondered where Tanja was, but she'd assumed that she had got up to dance and then gone to sit at another table.

As the nightclub emptied Tanja's friends realised she was missing. They laughed at first — Tanja must have found someone and dropped her friends like hot potatoes — but it was soon discovered that Tanja's red leather jacket was still hanging in the cloakroom, alone in an empty row of hooks, like a question mark. One of her girlfriends asked the cloakroom attendant if he had seen Tanja. He didn't remember, not then or later. Tanja's friend went back into the club and tried to call her. A phone rang from the sofa they'd been sitting on.

The next morning the babysitter woke up. Tanja's daughters were asleep. The babysitter discovered she was the only adult in the apartment. She called Tanja's mobile phone. Tanja's hungover friend answered. They decided to report the matter to the police. The police took their statement and said that if Tanja hadn't returned by the end of the day from wherever she might have spent the night, they would file a missing persons report. Tanja didn't return. A report was filed.

Two days later there was a quarter-page photo of Tanja in the evening paper. The sight of it made me catch my breath. It felt as if a dull knife had sliced though my gut and a cold, round stone had rolled in and lodged there.

Tanja Metsäpuro looked like my mother. They both had thick, dark brown hair, Tanja's long, my mother's shoulder-length. They both had eyes that were a mix of green and blue and features that were delicate and symmetrical, a thin nose with a sharp tip, thin lips, but a smile that was broad and warm, and — if you wanted to see it — mysterious. The were both pleasant, even beautiful women in their early thirties, small, slender, and petite.

When she disappeared Tanja had been wearing a skintight white top, black, shiny leggings, and high-heeled leather sandals. I imagine that many men in the nightclub would have noticed her, but it was a long way from that to a criminal act. Especially since Tanja hadn't talked to anyone but her friends while they were in the club. At least not before midnight. No one knew what had happened after that.

Someone thought that Tanja might have said she didn't feel well. This led to the idea that she had gone outside to get some fresh air. She had done that in the past, so why not this time as well? The cloakroom attendant spiked that idea. He was sure that hadn't happened — no one in Tanja's group had gone in or out.

Then it was discovered that there was another way out of the club. There was a back door that the club staff used. It opened onto the car park behind the building. The police thought of all this as well, but much too late. The footage from the video surveillance camera had already been auto-deleted. There was no other solid evidence, and nothing that would have suggested that Tanja Metsäpuro had gone out of the back door for some fresh air, or for any other reason.

Tanja's case was given almost a page a day in the evening tabloids for several weeks. They dug everything up: her ex-husband's multiple bankruptcies, his failure to pay child support, the abuse charges and no-contact order that Tanja had brought against him and later dropped. But he had a watertight alibi. On the day she disappeared — in fact from two weeks before the day until a week after — he had been in the Helsinki jail. He had been a suspect in a case of abetting a drug offence. This led to rumours that Tanja herself had been involved in drugs.

The more I read, the more certain I became. And it wasn't just because of the similarities between the two disappearances, both cases unexpected and unexplained, both women single mothers with beautiful, suntanned faces. It also had to do with Henrik Saarinen.

I already knew a thing or two about Saarinen. I'd had two years to find out.

I knew where he lived, and where he worked, and I knew that he sometimes took another, less imposing car, and went out for night-time drives. When I told Ketomaa these facts he said that driving a car at night was not a crime, and that the most it could tell us about Saarinen was that he might suffer from insomnia. Besides, Ketomaa said, driving can help you think. You could pull yourself together; alone in a car you could be in the world and outside it at the same time.

Ketomaa also said that he felt bad for me. I knew he wasn't talking about my mother any more. He was talking about me, about my life, which he thought I was wasting.

Tanja Metsäpuro dropped out of the headlines a month later.

A couple on a long hike found a nice spot on the shore in the Uutela recreation area and spread a blanket to enjoy a sunny autumn morning and a well-earned picnic lunch. As they got their food and coffee out of their packs, they noticed something in the water. At first they both thought it was just something that looked like a person.

It was a person: a body that the waves had pushed up against the rocks.

Tanja Metsäpuro was floating naked in the water, badly swollen, rotted until she was nearly purple.

Only one thing separated her case from my mother's disappearance. She had been found.

SEPTEMBER 2013

The fragrance of fresh hyacinths filled the clean, well-lit room with the intoxicating illusion of spring. The sensation was powerful, as if the calendar and my own sense of the season were completely wrong. The chandeliers in the hall were lit, the black tray on the table contained an assortment of refreshments. I did as I was asked. I sat on the sofa and waited, watching the ice cubes melt in a crystal goblet.

I'd taken a shower and come to the main house at the agreed time. I'd met Enni, seen the satisfaction and pride in her eyes and heard the happy tone in her voice. After a moment of chat she had put her hand on my shoulder and given it a few pats; I could still feel the warmth of her palm through my oxford shirt. The last thing she'd said was that it would go fine if I refrained from witticisms.

I'd smiled at her, thanked her for the advice, and wondered what she would think if I told her Henrik Saarinen murdered my mother.

The time would come.

Even for that.

Surrounded as I was by the subdued colours, dark wood furniture, silver candlesticks, and sparkling circles of crystal on the ceiling, the last ten years with all their twists and turns suddenly felt like another life, or like something that happened long ago. My mouth was dry, from thirst or other causes. I reached out to open a bottle of mineral water.

I heard steps. Relaxed and purposeful steps, coming down the stairs.

I pulled my hand back, got up from the sofa and stepped towards the antique table in the centre of the room. I'd been waiting twenty years, and I didn't exactly know what for. Was I about to look into the eyes of evil and know it, or would my journey prove a waste of time, my instinct wrong, my obsession at an unhappy, anticlimactic end?

Henrik Saarinen stepped into the brilliant, slightly golden glow of the chandeliers wearing a sunny smile. I don't know what I felt. I know that I felt none of the certainty I'd had for the past ten years. But I didn't need to. Everything didn't have to happen instantaneously. I'd waited twenty years, I could wait a little longer.

Saarinen looked exactly as I'd thought he would, powerful and charismatic. His presence filled the room and exuded the calm of inexhaustible certainty. He was dressed in expensive blue jeans, a white oxford shirt and a blue sweater with a little laughing crocodile on the breast. He was wearing soft leather slippers on his feet, no doubt expensive and comfortable.

His first two words were, "Henrik Saarinen."

I took hold of his outstretched hand. It was large and warm.

"Aleksi."

His release of my hand was as soft as his grasp. He looked at me through round-lensed glasses and pointed at the sofa. My eyes lingered on his perhaps longer than was natural.

"Drink?"

"Mineral water, thanks," I said.

Saarinen opened two bottles of water and pushed one in front of me. Then he seemed to think again and walked to the serving table next to the wall and poured himself a whisky from a green bottle. He returned to the sofa with a thick crystal glass in his hand.

"You have your first week behind you," he said, taking a taste from his glass. "How does it look?"

I filled my own glass with mineral water. It bubbled and fizzed against the ice as if in excitement.

"The work is interesting. The surroundings are beautiful. I've been enjoying myself."

"That's good. I've always thought that work should be interesting. Here's to that."

We drank. My mouth was so dry that it felt as if the water was reviving it from the dead.

"You've met Elias. And Enni, of course," Saarinen said, facing the window. The sun was setting. Soon even the glow of red and violet on the horizon would fade and everything would be black. "And perhaps Amanda?"

"Yes," I said. I wondered if I should mention our dinner, and decided not to. "I understand she enjoys fishing."

Saarinen put his glass on the table.

"And what about the grounds? What do you think of them?"

"Everything seems to be in good condition. Next spring you might think about refurbishing the eaves and rain gutters, but that's something to decide once winter is over. As far as the windows —"

"What about the feel of the place?"

"The feel of it? It feels very pleasant. Like the seaside. Peaceful."

"I agree. I bought it for the location, years ago. I thought I would sell the place if I got a good offer. But then I realised that somewhere like this could be very useful. In a way I had never appreciated before. As you can imagine."

He sat on the sofa like a king and looked at me from behind his glasses. I didn't want to say what I could imagine.

"I'm talking about solitude," Saarinen said, his eyes holding mine.

"Of course."

"That's why I wanted to meet you in person as soon as I could," he said, smiling. His smile was like the one on his shirt's green crocodile, ready to bite.

"Of course."

"Elias said that you signed the contract without any questions."

I nodded.

"So you understand the nature of the job as well as its duties."

"I believe so."

74

Saarinen took another sip and looked up at me again. I looked at his arms, his hands, each of his fingers. They were large-boned, thick, sturdy hands, his fingers long, and no doubt powerful.

"This is important," he said. "It's a delicate matter. You see, I've had bad experiences . . . with people who try to get near me and turn out to be something other than they've claimed to be."

He gave me a meaningful look. I took a drink of water. He did the same with his whisky. Noises drifted in from the kitchen. They sounded far away.

"The previous caretaker was a person like that. A very unpleasant fellow."

This was the first time I'd heard anything about my predecessor. Elias Ahlberg had simply said curtly that his employment had been terminated.

"What was his name?" I asked.

"It doesn't matter."

"Was he a local man, or was he from Helsinki, like —"

"It's not important."

Saarinen sipped his whisky.

"He seemed at first like a reliable sort. Older than you. We thought that was a good thing. Life experience, the wisdom of age, something like that. Everything went well at first. Then his less admirable qualities, shall we say deficiencies, and weaknesses, and so on, gained the upper hand. I'm sure you understand what I mean."

Did I understand? How many weaknesses could a person have? Thousands, no doubt. In this instance I imagined it was one of seven ways a man could get himself into trouble. My guess was greed, in case Saarinen was expecting an answer to his question.

"Age doesn't always bring wisdom," he said, pursing his whiskyed lips. "So we decided that the next caretaker should be young, fresh. And we hired you."

"A lucky break for me," I said, and meant it. "I've wanted a job like this for a long time."

Saarinen smiled.

"Attitude shouldn't be underestimated. I know that from experience. I wouldn't be here if attitude didn't matter. You should know what you want in life, and you should be willing to do whatever it takes to get it."

His gaze cooled.

"Do you know what you want?"

"Pretty well."

"Good," he said, lifting his glass to his lips again. "Some people drift. Never take their lives in their own hands. They don't understand that it's a struggle between the weak and the strong. Always. Every time. Bumbling amateurishness . . . The previous caretaker was an example of that."

"Of what?" I asked, when Saarinen didn't continue.

He didn't answer right away. He was still looking at me, but as if from a distance.

"A long week," he said. "Is there anything that comes to mind that you'd like to ask about, anything you need to know?"

Why did you take a little boy's mother away from him?

76

It was the first thing that occurred to me. It came to mind naturally and spontaneously. A man sitting on the sofa. His words, the weight of his voice, his presence. I still didn't feel the absolute certainty inside me that I'd felt twelve years earlier, but I felt something like it. Without even trying. It was all happening, on its own.

"No," I said, putting my glass down. "I don't think so. The work will teach the worker."

"Excellent. I'll go in to dinner. Good night."

Saarinen got up nimbly from the sofa and headed towards the kitchen and dining room. I had gone as far as the doorway when I heard, or sensed, something. I turned. Saarinen was facing me. He was standing straight across the room from me. I remembered what I'd felt when I saw him turn on television. This time I hadn't even seen that quick pivot, but I had known it, felt it happening.

"There was one interesting detail in your paperwork, by the way."

A cold wind went through me. There's no cause for panic, I told myself. You knew this moment would come. Saarinen doesn't know who you are. Everything's fine. Your papers are in order. Of course they are. A coolheaded administrator like Elias Ahlberg wouldn't have hired me if they weren't.

"You have no family at all," Saarinen said. "No people to contact if anything happens."

"Let's hope nothing happens."

Saarinen looked at me. The distance between us was ten or twelve metres, yet it felt as if he could easily lay a hand on my shoulder, touch me somehow.

"All right, then," he said. "That's what we'll do."

As he turned and walked away his shadow followed along the wall and into the other rooms of the house.

APRIL 2008

"I can't do it," Ketomaa said. "The police don't turn over that kind of material to just anyone. And no offence, but you are just anyone. It doesn't matter that it's been fifteen years since your mother's death. Even if it were longer, I still couldn't do it."

We hadn't seen each other in three years. Ketomaa had lost weight. The sturdy knot in his dark-blue necktie looked noticeably wider. His face was an older, furrowed Buster Keaton, as if the screen legend's famous stony face had been elongated and his cheeks and forehead had been gathered in deep folds just to accentuate his overall dryness, the absence of water, and life.

Ketomaa was wearing a hat though we were indoors, because the cancer treatment had claimed the last bit of hair on his head. The intelligent, probing look in his eyes was luckily unchanged. I didn't know quite why, but it felt good to see him again. Maybe this frail old policeman was the last remaining link to my past, to who and what I once was.

We had intended to have lunch at Juttutupa, which was nearby, but we'd left without ordering. Ketomaa said there was no point. His food would just sit on his plate. So we were sitting in the back room of the Rytmi coffee shop.

On the other side of the room a young man tapped at a laptop. His head of blond curls rocked in rhythm and now and then, after a particularly furious bout of typing, he would give a little nod. Outside the large window the usual assortment of drug addicts, office workers, hipsters and locals went up and down Toinen linja. The spring weather made everything limpid and bright.

"I knew you would say that. Just thought I'd ask. And there's something else I wanted to talk to you about."

"Let me guess," Ketomaa said quietly. He knew how to speak in such a way that you could only hear him if you were sitting directly in front of him. "Tanja Metsäpuro. The answer is the same."

"I don't need the files. I just want to know where they are with it. It disappeared from the papers a long time ago."

"Let it disappear," Ketomaa sighed. "The case is going nowhere."

"Tell me about it."

"I don't know if that would be wise. I don't mean for me. I'm talking about you. It's nice to see you and see that you at least appear to be doing well. But . . . Neither one of us is getting any younger. Life is so short; you should use it for what matters."

"Tanja Metsäpuro," I said.

"You would have made a good cop," Ketomaa said, and laughed dryly. He shoved his hat further back on his head and thought for a moment. "A good cop who wasted his life on hopeless cases. Chasing unsolved crimes his whole career, his whole life, and forgetting about little things like family, children, happiness, companionship, and not noticing until the end of his life that it was all a waste. This isn't second-hand knowledge for me."

He looked at me, then at the street, then turned his face to me again.

"All right," he sighed. "What you do with it is your own responsibility. It's your life. I don't really know what's happening with the case, I'm not personally involved in it, but of course I hear a thing or two. As I'm sure you deduced from the newspapers, it started with the body. But then no other evidence turned up. They've tried every angle."

He sipped his lemon soda and looked at me almost expectantly.

"Eventually they arrested her ex-husband as a suspect."

"The one who was in jail when it happened?"

Ketomaa tugged at his collar.

"The idea was that it all had to do with drugs. That the crime was meant to send a message. That's their strongest theory at this point. That's all I can tell you. I've already told you more than I ought to. Chalk it up to the radiation. What do you say? Are you satisfied?"

"Of course not."

"Of course not. How did I guess."

We sat silent for a moment. The young writer put on headphones. They were large and black and covered half his head, leaving just his rosy, eager nose, soft, boyish cheeks, red-pimpled chin, and bountiful curls sticking out in every direction. His fingers hammered on the keys.

"Did Tanja Metsäpuro know Henrik Saarinen?"

Ketomaa's expression didn't waver. I repeated the question. He leaned back. His suit jacket looked almost empty.

"Aleksi, can I tell you something?"

"Did she know —"

"I've been thinking about this disease," he said. His arms were crossed over his chest, his face open and innocent. "Thinking about what cancer is. Cancer cells spread without understanding that by spreading they're destroying the thing they live in. Their greed is like that, endless. They're killing themselves. They destroy, only to be destroyed." The lemon soda rose from the table and disappeared between his lips. "Given a choice, why would you do that?"

And what if you have no choice, I wanted to ask. What if the choice was made for you? I didn't say anything for a moment. Ketomaa's question hung between us. I took a sip of coffee and waited. Ketomaa looked at me again.

"So you don't want to answer my question, but I'm supposed to answer yours."

"It's important to me," I said.

"I'm not sure."

"It's not going to kill you."

"It's a fifty-fifty chance."

His face continued unflinchingly expressionless. Finally he spoke.

"Yes. Tanja had been seeing Henrik Saarinen."

"Christ," I said. "I could have told you a thousand years ago that you ought to arrest Saarinen."

Ketomaa suddenly looked absolutely furious and frustrated. I didn't remember ever seeing him like that.

"I'm only telling you this so you'll come to your senses. Their connection ended about six months before she disappeared. And it wasn't a close connection even before that. It was one of those things between an older, richer man and a younger woman."

"Says who?"

"The police had a chat with Saarinen, of course."

"They had a chat with him. What the fuck did they chat about? Why not arrest him and convict him?"

Ketomaa opened his mouth a couple of times as if he was gulping for air.

"My mouth gets so dry these days."

He poured some more soda in his mouth as if he were watering a tender plant, and said, "Of course they didn't just chat with him. They investigated everything and kept all their options open as long as possible. They looked at Tanja's phone records and emails and everything they'd collected in their investigation, all the depositions and reports, they combed through everything. People were brought in for more questioning."

He leaned forward and set his elbows on the table, his eyes drilling into me.

"And there was nothing. Nada. Not one meeting for the whole six months. There was no trace of Henrik Saarinen in Tanja Metsäpuro's life."

He leaned closer.

"Do you understand, Aleksi? Do you understand what I'm saying?"

I looked at him. "You have a 50 per cent chance of survival. That probably doesn't sound like a lot. But if you compare that to a 20 per cent chance, it's a hell of a lot. And if you compare it to zero, it's a gift from heaven." I paused for a heartbeat and asked, "Do you understand what *I'm* saying?"

SEPTEMBER 2013

After meeting Henrik Saarinen I couldn't sleep. Naturally. The past was a bramble, dense and thick with thorns.

My little room and kitchen felt cramped and unfamiliar. The night sky outside the window was brilliantly cloudless, the stars bright as approaching aeroplanes. The floorboards let out low creaks as I paced from the foot of the bed to the kitchen and back again. I finally tired of walking, made some tea, and sat down at the table.

Twenty years, and where was I?

At a moment like that I wished I could produce some file, some written document that would have justified me, strengthened my theories, something I could have examined for some compelling detail, some important insight. There was no such document. It was all between my ears. It was all in what I believed, what I knew, what I had been able to find out, deduced, pondered. Now and then I would get hold of that certainty that I'd felt twelve years earlier. Now and then I would know what that conviction felt like.

I knew that Henrik Saarinen liked women who looked like my mother. I'd seen pictures of him in the papers. After his marriage ended he had appeared publicly with at least ten different women, and half of them reminded me of my mother in some way. I knew that Saarinen had owned Simola, the mid-sized shipping company where my mother had worked. I knew that my mother had sat in on meetings led by Saarinen. I knew that my mother had met someone who had wanted to keep his identity secret. I knew one or two things about Saarinen's life and habits. I knew that he had a dark side, but I had no concrete evidence of anything.

Henrik Saarinen had also disappeared from the public eye.

His transformation from social lion to low-profile investor and man behind the scenes had happened in two phases. The first shift occurred when a young woman brought charges against him for assault. The woman, a star of reality television, had left a nightclub with two other women and gone to Saarinen's apartment in Eira to continue their night's revels. When they arrived at his building on Tehtaankatu something happened. The two other women went home, leaving the young woman alone with Saarinen and, according to her, Saarinen's behaviour then changed completely. He tore off her clothes and began whipping her with a belt, forcing her to kneel in front of him and ordering her to lick his shoes. She tore herself from his grasp, struck him with a lamp from the bedside table, and escaped to the street. She immediately told her story to a tabloid and later withdrew the charges. The incident nevertheless had its effect on Saarinen. A photo was taken of him with one eye swollen and a bandage over his injured cheek, through which could be seen a dark row of stitches that indicated more than a minor scratch.

The second change occurred a little later, just before Tanja Metsäpuro's disappearance. Saarinen's longtime trustee, the CEO of one of his holdings and an old friend of his, resigned his post and moved to Germany. Neither man would give any comment on the matter and the reason for the break was never made public. Following these events, Saarinen withdrew from the headlines completely.

I looked out into the night and thought about Henrik Saarinen sleeping just a hundred metres away while I sat awake. After twenty years I was a stone's throw from the man who had the answers to my questions. All I needed to do was find a way to ask, and do whatever was required to get an answer.

I wanted to find my mother. I wanted to say goodbye. I wanted to know what happened on that October evening twenty years ago, and why. I wanted answers.

An ache crept up my shoulders and neck to my temples. I gently massaged them. I decided to get up and take an aspirin and have a snack and try to get some sleep, even if it meant nightmares. I rubbed the sides of my head with my fingertips, and didn't hear the creak of footsteps on the stairway until they were just outside my apartment door. I heard a knock, short and polite, and looked at the clock on the microwave. The red display said 00:51. I got up from the chair and walked to the door. Without turning on the light or asking who was there, I opened it. I knew who it was.

Amanda stood in the starlight, her face in shadow, and said, "Guess how I knew you weren't asleep."

"I have no idea."

"You met my father."

I stepped aside.

"Would you like a cup of tea? I don't have anything stronger."

"A cup of tea would be good."

She came inside and stood in the middle of the room. I went to the little kitchen, filled the kettle, and flipped the switch. I pointed to the wooden chair on the other side of the table. Amanda sat down. She was dressed in white sneakers, straight-legged jeans, and a black leather jacket.

"Is this what you do?" she asked. "Sit in the dark all night?"

"The light switch is behind you."

"This is fine."

The sound of the kettle was like a dozen wheezing radiators. I took a mug from one cupboard and a teabag in its packet from another and set them on the table in front of her. She looked around the room. Her eyes were obviously adjusted to the darkness and she could see what I saw: one room with a kitchen, simple furnishings, a pile of books, and few possessions. She looked at me again.

"Pretty stripped down."

"It's not exactly *House and Garden*."

Her eyes shone bright in the starlight. She laid her right hand on the table and pressed her fingers against the tea packet as if she were checking to be sure there was a teabag inside. I was still standing in the kitchen doorway, waiting for the kettle to boil.

"I go too far when I'm drinking sometimes . . . All those stories. Drunken nonsense. I gave you completely the wrong idea about myself."

The water started to boil. I picked up the kettle and poured two mugs full. The rising steam was blue in the starlight and looked solid somehow, as if you could grab it and open your fist to see what it was made of.

"Don't worry," I said. "I'm not going to think about it."

"This probably doesn't look too smart, either. Coming here in the middle of the night."

She dipped the teabag into her mug, then picked it up with the spoon I slid across the table. She moved the mug and the steam followed it like a dog.

"You must think my life is pretty pitiful," she said.

"I don't know anything about your life."

"Except everything. I told you everything. It's been weighing on me all day. But not just that. There's something else, too."

"I noticed you went out early this morning."

Amanda's blue-grey eyes peered out from dark mascara. It was the middle of the night and her make-up was perfect, her hair sleek and shining. As I looked at her I understood what had happened on the shore. Why I had stood on the dock in the cold wind and rain, looking out to sea. For the same reason that I'd just opened the door and invited her in.

"I drove to Helsinki and thought I would spend the weekend there. Or what's left of it. Then I changed my mind." She sipped her tea. "I haven't had anything to drink today."

"OK."

"Not that I need to explain anything to you."

She leaned back in her chair, crossed her arms on her chest, and turned towards the window. It was so quiet that I could hear the earthquake rumble of the refrigerator.

"Do you believe in coincidences?" she asked.

"It depends."

She smiled and looked at me again. She put her hands down on the table.

"I've always thought that was an either-or question."

"If I have to choose, I'd say no. I don't believe in coincidences."

"Neither do I."

She got up from her chair, and so did I. We met in the middle of the room. Her lips tasted like salt, lipstick, and the mint aftertaste of chewing gum. Her breath was heavy and trembling. She felt heavenly, and absolutely wrong.

AUGUST 1993

Outside it's a clear day, the sun high in a blue, cloudless sky. It must be Saturday because on any other day we would have gone to the library in the evening, after my mother got home from work. The only other person in the library is the librarian, sitting at her desk staring motionless at the library door. When you pull a book from the shelf a cloud of dust motes hangs in the air for a second, twinkling like stars, then immediately disappears somewhere.

My mother has books large and small and magazines in front of her. She's sitting in the middle of a puddle of brilliant light, and she looks upset. I've never seen her like that. The library is quiet as a mouse, so her frantic flipping through the pages of each book and magazine one after another sounds loud. She tucks her thick, auburn hair behind her ear and looks completely absorbed in what she's doing. She moves the middle and index finger of her right hand from a magazine page to a book's page and back as if she were marking them with an invisible pencil.

I watch her first from a distance, among the shelves, and then walk over to her. She's wearing a light-blue shirt that almost glows in the dazzling light. Her eyes are wide open, questioning — she's found what she was looking for.

What are you doing? I ask.

She doesn't answer, continues reading, making her invisible marks. I ask again. Now she looks up at me, but her mind is still on her reading. She notices this, too, blinks a few times, and smiles.

I'm looking for something.

What?

The magazines on the table are filled with boring charts and black and white diagrams that look as if they were drawn with badly shaking hands. I can tell that they're statistics. They have to do with my mother's work. One of the magazines is different. It's illustrated and has large photographs of people. Some of the people have drinks in their hands. They're all smiling. Some have white teeth that make it look as if there's a hole in the paper where their mouths are and underneath is the whitest white paper.

It's something my mother's interested in.

My mother's voice is different in the library. Quiet but very clear. I look at the photo spread again.

Do you know them? I ask, meaning the people with the drinks in their hands, who seem to be laughing and smiling about something I can't grasp.

At first she doesn't seem to have understood my question. Then she looks at the picture in front of her.

God, no, she says, and closes the magazine, and I see the picture on the cover. It's a picture of a man in a dark suit and red necktie, with a well-groomed face and round glasses. He's looking at the camera like he knows what the photographer is thinking.

My mother stares at the picture. It's as if she's expecting the man to say something. He doesn't say anything. The light falls on her like rain.

I have a copy of that magazine. Not the same copy she was reading, of course, but that's not important. What's important is the August 1993 issue, and the man on the cover is Henrik Saarinen.

SEPTEMBER 2013

The pillow smelled like Amanda, and it still had the imprint of her head, and a few black hairs. I got up and opened the window a crack. The tart, cool air of an autumn Sunday morning rushed in as if it was blown through a nozzle. The sun was up and the part of the sky I could see through the window was glowing blue. I put the coffee on to brew and went back to bed. Fresh air flooded into the room. It was quiet, and I was alone.

Sunday was officially my day off, a day I could use as I saw fit. Not that anyone outside work had been waiting somewhere for me on any of the other days. My phone rang very rarely and when it did it was usually about the care and upkeep of the estate. I didn't really have any friends, and certainly not any I would see or talk to on the phone regularly.

I was thinking about Amanda. About how I had itched for her without admitting it to myself, how I'd acted on my desire at the worst possible time with the worst possible person.

Twelve years of diligent work deliberately, knowingly and utterly mucked up. Twelve years living with one goal absolutely firm in my mind, denying myself a lot of things, taking risks, watching my back. And then, on one starry night, I'd gone and done something that could send the whole thing toppling.

Amanda excited me, attracted me. It was the same irrational attraction that I'd suffered for in the past — the wrong women, wrong decisions, rotten results. Amanda was one of those blind spots where my brain stopped working, where the rush and tumult of the body blocked out everything that rationality and instinct was telling me.

I got up and poured myself some coffee.

My meeting with Henrik Saarinen the evening before replayed in my mind. I tried to put it into a clear form, to go through the conversation in the order that it happened, what was left unsaid, what was clearly stated.

But memory doesn't work that way. Events don't arrange themselves in a logical chain, like a scene in a movie. The kind of movie I would have liked to watch again and again, finding new meanings, new possibilities, logical connections. Even if I did manage to see the events as they actually happened, without adding anything or leaving anything out, it would only work one time. The very next time I thought about it my memory would light up with new connections, with other memories of other times, and the puzzle would be in pieces again.

But I had seen something. Something that confirmed that I was on the right track, that my instinct twelve years before had been right, in some measure, at least. Henrik Saarinen's hands, his voice, his body language. His past, my mother's interest in him. An interest that I had reason to believe was broad and deep. And my mother's past, of course. It all led to the thought that was always with me, that I rarely wanted to put into words, even though it was what was behind my decision to come: the thought that I might find my mother here, on the grounds of this estate, buried in the woods or at the bottom of the sea.

The thought was both horrifying and comforting. I closed the window and poured the last bit of cold coffee into the sink, watching as the thick, black liquid formed its own dark whirlpool in the clear water from the tap, tenaciously clinging to its colour before vanishing.

I found a sheltered spot on the shore. The sea sparkled so brightly that I could only look at it for a few seconds at a time. I closed my eyes, turned towards the sun, and tried my best to relax. The warmth and light fell on my face softly, slowly, as if poured with a sure, steady hand. The nearby woods were humming and little waves were splashing on the beach, but if I'd imagined that my dark thoughts would be left in my small apartment, I was wrong.

My mind kept returning to recent events, searching for something significant, for explanations, possible reasons for what had happened over the past couple of days. In spite of the fact that I was sitting under a vaulting sky next to a boundless sea basking in gentle sunlight, I was in a dark, cramped space. That was nothing new. I'd spent years in that space, wanting to break out. I breathed in, opened my eyes, and saw a man I recognised on the dock.

The chauffeur, Markus Harmala, was bringing something down to the motorboat, apparently planning to go for a pleasant autumn outing. He had a wheelbarrow filled with supplies and was unloading its contents into the cabin and onto the deck of the boat. I watched him and recognised his movements. Because I had been following Henrik Saarinen for some years, I had of course also been following Markus Harmala. In fact you could say it was really Harmala who was being followed, since he was driving.

Watching him now after such a long time, he wasn't necessarily Saarinen's evil and annoying appendage. He looked like a man who had been sitting for hundreds of hours in his boss's company, shut up in the same car. He looked like a man who knew Henrik Saarinen.

I got up and walked to the dock. Harmala didn't notice me coming. He lifted a black plastic box out of the wheelbarrow, jumped onto the boat, and looked into the cabin. I waited. After a moment he climbed back onto the dock.

"Good morning," I said, stretching out my hand. "Aleksi Kivi, the caretaker."

Harmala looked like a rich man's driver. He was colourless and neat. Blue eyes, blond hair parted on the side and combed, a small chin. He was thin and of medium height, and I had noticed that his neutral-toned, fashionable clothing sat on him as if he had chosen an age and finally grown to fit it. He was about five years older than me.

"Markus Harmala," he said. His handshake was quick and polite. He didn't say that he was the chauffeur. Maybe he had the day off, too.

"Planning a long trip?" I asked.

Harmala glanced at the boat. He had a light-brown mole on his right cheek the size and shape of the head of a screw. It underlined the neutrality, the invisibility of the rest of his features.

"What do you mean?"

"You've got a lot of provisions. Are you waiting for Henrik?"

"My boss?" he said, and sounded genuinely bewildered. The bewilderment didn't last long. "No, I'm waiting for Amanda."

"The two of you going?" I heard myself ask, then realised immediately that I'd given in to an impulse, like I had the night before. That was all I needed, to be jealous of Amanda and not even be aware of it.

"That's what it looks like," Harmala said. Something happened. Something changed in his eyes. Maybe his face froze for a split second. "Unless we have unexpected guests."

The wheelbarrow still contained some cardboard boxes filled with an assortment of wine, both white and red. Harmala didn't say anything for a moment. His blue eyes were opaque, no depth.

"You're the new caretaker. Of course. I guess I wasn't listening, didn't put it together. Slow on the uptake. Glitch in the ignition. Sorry. Must have been lost in my thoughts."

He said this in a voice that wasn't quite convincing to the listener. He nodded towards the shore.

"What do you think? Of the place."

Why does everyone here ask the same question?

"I've only been here a week. Seems like an interesting place in many ways."

"A week?" Harmala said, looking at me as if calculating something. "I thought . . . OK. Welcome. I've been here for more than ten years, since 2002."

"So you know the place well."

He lifted a box from the wheelbarrow, the bottles clinking together.

"Like the inside of my own pocket," he said.

"Great. I might ask your advice sometime, or get your help with something."

"Sure," he said, his voice noncommittal, then turned, stepped into the boat, and disappeared into the cabin. The trees all along the shore bent their tops in the wind. Aside from the splashing of the waves it was completely quiet. I looked at the boat. The cabin windows reflected myself and the dock and the water. But more importantly, a feeling.

I was being watched.

The wind had turned cold again.

Harmala soon came back onto the dock. His light-coloured jeans, white tennis shoes, and dark blue Henry Lloyd warm-up jacket made him look like a member of a yacht club.

"What did you say your name was?" he asked.

"Aleksi Kivi."

"Really? Isn't that the writer?"

"That's Aleksis Kivi, with an s on the end. My mother was an avid reader of Finnish literature."

"Have we met before?"

"Never."

I didn't have to lie. We had never met. I had just followed him for miles by car and on foot whenever he was with Saarinen. He took hold of the wheelbarrow handles and thought for a moment.

"Who interviewed you?"

"Elias Ahlberg."

"Of course. I've got to go and get the rest of the stuff. It was nice to meet you. See you around."

The wheels of the barrow bumped over the boards of the dock until he reached the shore and then were silent.

"See you," I said.

I walked for an hour in the woods and around the grounds. When I got back to the house and my apartment I cleaned and did the laundry. I lay in bed and read a book. Now and then I got up and looked out of the window. I didn't like my thoughts, what I was feeling, who my mind kept returning to.

The evening darkened and the sun crept to the horizon in varied hues of red. The strip of sky turned pink for a moment, then almost immediately a deep violet, and then the horizon was gone.

At ten-thirty I fell asleep.

Henrik Saarinen and Markus Harmala left early on Monday morning. I didn't see Amanda. Enni got in her dark blue Škoda around noon, said she wouldn't be back until Saturday evening, and drove away. I did my day's work under a cloudless sky in still autumn weather and ate dinner in the kitchen of the main house. After dinner I walked from one quiet room to the next and ended up in the library. I turned on a lamp, looked at the books on the shelves, and eventually sat down in an imposing leather armchair. The leather was brown, worn soft as flannel in places. It quickly warmed under me. My phone rang and I took it out of my pocket.

"Hello Aleksi."

Ketomaa's voice sounded familiar and far away. There was something touching about it. It felt like a memory that you know you have but don't want to let into the light of day, because you know it will be painful, will turn out to be something other than what you think.

"Hello."

"Am I calling at a bad time?" Ketomaa asked.

"Not at all," I said. "I've got my feet up."

Ketomaa cleared his throat.

"It's been a while. Months. How are you?"

"Very good."

"Very good? That's all?"

"Yep," I said.

"Are you sure?" Ketomaa said, and I didn't need him to explain what he meant. I wondered what he would say if I told him about my job. Or that I was sitting in Henrik Saarinen's library. I'd often thought since I'd come here that at some point I would have to tell

Ketomaa where I was and what I'd found out. If I did find anything out. If not, there would be no reason to tell him.

"Are you getting used to being retired?"

"It has its good side. At first I wondered what the hell I was going to do with all my time, of course, but my days seem to fill up. Either that or I'm slowing down. A trip to the barber's takes all day. But I suppose I should be grateful I have some business to give a barber."

"Indeed," I said.

"And I haven't completely given up investigating," Ketomaa said. "A little exercise keeps the mind alert. I'm freelancing these days. Doing some work for insurance companies and individuals."

I didn't say anything.

"Of course it's mostly following unfaithful wives and husbands and catching insurance scammers, but I think of it as a hobby. Or I guess hobby's the wrong word, since it pays more than police work ever did, if you count it by the hour."

He was quiet for a moment. Maybe he was waiting for me to say something.

"It sounds as if everything's going well," I said. "That's good to hear."

As I spoke my eyes wandered over the bookshelves. They stopped at a thin volume of poetry.

"Are you still working as a carpenter?" I heard Ketomaa ask.

I got up from the chair and took two steps towards the bookshelves. They were full, but well-organised. On the shelf at eye-level were several books of poems.

102

"Hello?"

My gaze fastened on a thin, blue-covered book. I reached for it, and only understood my own words once they were out of my mouth.

"A caretaker."

I stopped. Ketomaa didn't speak for a second.

"A caretaker?" he asked.

How had I lost the thread for that second? What had happened to my mind? It was a feeling like the one I'd had at that moment in front of the television long ago, and a few days ago sitting across from Saarinen.

A dark room that I had to get out of.

I took hold of the book. My hands were shaking. The book, not much larger than a wallet, fell to the floor with a slap.

"Aleksi, are you all right?"

I picked up the book.

"You said you're a caretaker? Where?"

His voice had taken on that all-too-familiar tone. Somewhere between teacher and scold, with more than a touch of I *expected more from you*. I put the book on the table. Ketomaa must under no circumstances know where I was. I knew what he might do. Come here, blow my cover, thinking it was for my own good, that he was helping me.

"Sorry," I said. "I was just thinking about my building caretaker. I need to get in touch with him."

Ketomaa was silent for a moment.

"Aleksi, It was my job to listen to people lie for forty years. I'm familiar with all the variations. Fibs, white lies, half-truths, and bald-faced falsehoods. That last

103

one can be ruled out in your case. What does that leave us?"

I tried to concentrate.

"Honest," I said. "I'm doing the same work I've always done. Carpentry. Repairs and renovations."

There was a low sigh on the other end of the line, like the steady leak from a tyre.

"Fine," Ketomaa finally said. "Doing what you've always done. Got it."

The book's cover was familiar. I remembered seeing it on my mother's bedside table. Of course you could find Eino Leino's poems in almost any Finnish home, but this edition was a rarer one. There were scuffs on the cover that I seemed to recognise.

"Same as always," I said.

Why were my fingers trembling? I opened the thin volume, flipped through it. Familiar underlines in thin, black, ballpoint pen.

> Ken yhtä ihmistä rakastaa,
> se kaikkia rakastaapi.
> Ken kerran voi itsensä unhoittaa,
> se unten onnen saapi.
>
> He who loves one other soul
> will love all others, too,
> And he who once forgets himself
> will make his dreams come true

"Aleksi?"
"Yeah?"

"Should we meet sometime?"

I turned to the first page.

Thin, black ballpoint pen.

Sonja Merivaara. My mother.

"Aleksi?"

I hung up the phone, sat down in the chair. I opened the book to a random page. One lone underline.

. . . dark as my heart . . .

I couldn't swallow, couldn't speak.

I was driving well above the speed limit. My new Volvo V60 could easily do 180 km/h. The night was dark on either side of the road, the lit asphalt like a tunnel in space.

I knew that it might all be a coincidence. My mother's possessions, including her books, had all been donated somewhere. It might very well be that some of her books had ended up at a second-hand bookshop and were now owned by many people. And since it was twenty years ago, the book I'd found might have changed hands several times.

I looked at the book on the passenger seat. One of my mother's favourites. A book she had written her own name in. Handwriting I would have known anywhere, at any time, from just one word. I remembered something Amanda had said.

Do you believe in coincidences?

No. Not now, if I ever really did.

I passed two lorries.

My hands weren't shaking any more. My eyes were dry. My foot on the accelerator was relaxed and sure.

I knew that Ketomaa would get in touch with me again soon. I knew he meant well. I was further along than ever before, closer than ever, but still with such a slender thread that it wouldn't be proof to anyone but me. I could almost see Ketomaa's exasperated, weary look if I saw him and pulled the book out of my pocket and showed him my mother's name. I could almost hear what he would say.

The man collects books. That's not a crime.

I braked a little to avoid rear-ending a bus. It took half a minute to carefully pass it. When the bus finally slid back into its lane like a boat into a slip, I floored the accelerator again.

JUNE 2013

I saw Ketomaa a few months before I started working at Henrik Saarinen's estate. I'd been quizzed by Elias Ahlberg twice and it looked as if I was going to be their choice for caretaker. I didn't mention the job to Ketomaa. We had more important things to talk about. At least I thought we did.

"Every ten years?" Ketomaa said.

"My mother disappeared in 1993," I said. "Tanja Metsäpuro disappeared, was murdered, in 2003."

Ketomaa gave me a sideways glance. We were walking in Kaisaniemi Park. In the pure, leafy green, the park's reputation for rape and robbery felt like a distant possibility.

"Where to begin," Ketomaa said. "Maybe with the fact that there is no indication of a connection between the two cases. And before you say anything, of course I understand that you see such a connection. Your mother and Tanja Metsäpuro were the same age, of similar appearance, and a few other weak links would otherwise seem to connect them, but that's a far cry from proof of a single perpetrator, let alone one who acted in any systematic way. It's purely theoretical . . ."

He glanced at me again.

"And you look as if you're not telling me everything."

We came to a small side path with views over the bay to Siltasaari. The Baltic shone blue, the rays of the sun bouncing off the windows of the row of buildings on the shore. Ketomaa sat down on a park bench, and so did I. Half a metre of summer wind and fresh sea air lay between us.

"I tried to tell you. This is 2013. Something's going to happen."

"Because you feel it will," Ketomaa said slowly.

"Yes."

"Can you tell me why?"

I leaned my back against the bench. Ketomaa was a man of facts, concrete realities. I wasn't going to tell him that there was something about the dates that seemed fateful, like it had when I'd seen Henrik Saarinen's golden-brown face on television. I arranged my words carefully.

"It takes time to find the right person. When the person is found, she can't be killed immediately. She has to be made to trust, to believe that they share a wonderful secret. She has to fall in love, to be full of hope. She has to be conquered. So that when the murder happens, it's all taken away from her. That's what gives Henr— . . . or whoever it is, satisfaction."

I turned towards Ketomaa as I spoke. He had a way of looking and listening that gave a person a peculiar feeling, as if someone were finally hearing every word your heart had to say. It was an old policeman's trick he had. For all I knew he could be thinking about the crossword in this morning's newspaper and all the while looking as if he was completely in the here and now.

"The ten years between my mother's disappearance and Tanja's murder isn't random. The victims were random, but not the time. He's systematic. He enjoys it. He's a man who sets goals and achieves them. He stays on schedule. The pressure of keeping to a timetable is part of the enjoyment. That pressure came to bear on Tanja's disappearance. You can see it in the crime in all sorts of ways."

Ketomaa's eyes were like two soft, blue pillows. I continued.

"You know what I'm talking about. You must remember the Hyvinkää case from the early nineties. The killer was never caught. That tells you that a person can do a thing like that and get away with it, come out without a scratch. That applies to my mother's disappearance even more than the Hyvinkää case. Because her body was never found. Another example of that kind of compulsion is that guy in Oulu who raped and strangled three women in exactly the same way, right after being released for the very same crime. This unknown person we're talking about, the one who murdered my mother and Tanja, shows the same behaviour. He does it because he has to, but since he's an organised, systematic person who's used to success, he doesn't act blindly, and he doesn't get caught."

Ketomaa looked out over the bay. A gust of wind wrinkled the water.

"I see you've boned up on these matters," he said. "In both of the cases you mention, your interpretation is correct, in a way."

A pair of wild ducks waddled up to our bench side by side and stopped a few metres off with deeply disappointed looks. They must have seen that we didn't have any bread.

"The Hyvinkää killer is either in jail for some other crime or dead," Ketomaa said. "Otherwise the crimes would have continued. That's clear. The guy in Oulu has a compulsion, of course. He's released after a few years and then he's compelled to rape and kill again. You don't have to be a detective or know much about their backgrounds to see what's happening. Anyone could understand it. In those cases. The problem with trying to connect these two cases is that you have to create facts that don't correspond to reality. It's a bit like taking your favourite scenes from two movies and trying to combine them to create a movie that perfectly suits your taste. The pieces won't fit together."

"What does correspond to reality? What would fit together? If there's nothing in the known facts that explains my mother's disappearance and Tanja's death, then there must be some explanation that hasn't occurred to anybody for some reason."

Ketomaa sighed.

"Every ten years," he said.

"I'm sure of it," I said.

He sharpened his gaze.

"So?"

"So what?"

"This is 2013. Don't tell me you haven't thought any further than that."

Should I tell him that I would soon be working on Henrik Saarinen's estate? Should I tell him about the certainty that had grown inside me? About the fact that deep down I was sure that in 2013 someone was going to die at the hands of the same man who had murdered my mother? Or rather, they would die, if someone didn't prevent it from happening.

I turned to look at the water and for the first time in my life I lied to Ketomaa.

"I haven't thought of anything else other than what I just told you."

SEPTEMBER 2013

Coming into Helsinki had always been a homecoming. I couldn't help but feel it. It didn't matter how long I'd been away or where I was coming from. When I passed Tarvaspää and Munkkiniemi on the highway from the north, it felt as if I'd made it safely through, as if I'd arrived. But the feeling would fade as quickly as it came over me. As I drove deeper into the city proper I usually didn't feel anything. Usually. This time I did. And it was not at all a joyful return.

I passed the Hietalahti shipyards, turned onto Tehtaankatu, parked in a paid spot and walked a few hundred metres. I could see the lights shining from the third floor of Saarinen's apartment. I took a few more quick steps towards the building and stopped. I stood on the odd-numbered side of the street and tried to sink into the shadows, towards the darkness. In front of the building, on the other side of the road, was Amanda's black, custom Range Rover.

The air was cool, the time nearly midnight. A couple came around a corner, a man and woman, probably in their forties, and expensively dressed. I felt their curious looks as they walked by, pausing in their conversation and continuing it once they were a safe distance past the strange man in the shadows.

As I looked up at the third floor I thought about my options, about what I'd decided on the drive here: I wasn't going to take my eyes off Saarinen again; I would dig the truth out of him no matter what it took.

A tram approached from the direction of the shipyards, sliding through the night, weirdly silent, and passing the empty tram stop as if in a dream.

The street door opened. I pressed deeper into the shadow of the courtyard passageway and watched as Amanda Saarinen stepped onto the street and headed towards her car. Right after her came a man whom I recognised as Markus Harmala. Amanda was wearing a short black dress and high heels. Her arms were bare in spite of the coolness of the night. She nearly ran to the car and Harmala followed.

Harmala glanced around. He was dressed in black leather shoes, black suit trousers, and a bright white, button-up shirt. Amanda was rummaging in her bag. Every other step she took was too short or too long. Harmala caught up with her and said something that I couldn't hear. Amanda swung her bag at his head. He easily dodged it and tore it out of her hands.

Harmala dug through the bag and apparently found what he was looking for. His hand went straight to his trouser pocket. He threw the bag back to Amanda and said something. I couldn't make out the words, but Amanda could. Her body stiffened, her back straightened, and she stood firmly on her feet. The hand holding her bag flew in a swift right jab.

Harmala must have been as surprised by her quickness and accuracy as I was. The first punch was followed by another, a hook this time, and the bag whacked Harmala in the face again, but she didn't surprise him the third time. He caught the flying bag in the air with his left hand, and raised his right.

"Hey!"

The shout came out of my mouth before I could think it through.

Harmala stopped and turned. I stepped onto the street. Amanda said something, but Harmala wasn't interested in her any more. His eyes were fixed on me. I stopped a few metres from the two of them. Harmala's eyes were impassive.

"The caretaker," he said. "This is a surprise. What are you doing here?"

"I came to pick up those brass fittings."

From close up, Amanda looked as if she had been enjoying herself. Not drunk, but not sober either.

"Brass fittings," Harmala said. "What brass fittings?"

"It's no big deal. I can get them any time," I said. I nodded to Amanda. "Everything all right?"

Harmala wasn't falling for my ruse. His eyes didn't let go of me.

"I asked you what you're doing here."

Amanda looked at me. She may have been smiling a little.

"Aleksi."

"Hi, Amanda," I said.

"This is quite a coincidence, wouldn't you say?" Harmala said. His voice was more insistent this time, hoarse and breathless.

"Anything I can help with?" I asked.

Harmala and I stared at each other for a moment. I counted the seconds. If I kept it up he would have only one option — to accept my explanation. Whether he believed my story or not was another matter. I smelled alcohol and perfume in the cold night air. Both coming from Amanda, I would guess.

"Sure," Harmala said finally, taking a step backwards. "You might drive this lady home."

Amanda smiled. Harmala smiled, too, but it was a fake smile. His voice had the same friendly veneer as when we'd met earlier.

"As you can see, Amanda's had a few today. And yesterday. And the day before."

I looked at her. She didn't seem nearly as drunk as his words would indicate.

"Shall we go, Amanda?" I said.

She looked at me, then at Harmala, but she didn't say anything. Harmala was still smiling his joyless smile.

"Thanks again for an unforgettable evening, Amanda. Your father must be pleased. This is just the kind of evening and the kind of company he craves."

"May I have the car keys?" I asked Harmala.

He gave me a questioning look.

"The car keys in your pocket," I said, "that you took out of Amanda's bag."

The smile disappeared from his face. I realised that I had misinterpreted the scene I'd just witnessed. Harmala hadn't come out to the street to prevent Amanda from driving drunk. He'd done it for some other reason. But what?

"The keys are in her bag," Harmala said. "If the lady wants to drive, it's up to her. It's none of my business. Here."

What is your business? I wondered. What's in her bag that is your business?

I took the bag from him, zipped it open, and found the keys. I beeped the doors open. Harmala had his smile back.

"I'll have to mention this to Henrik," he said as I took Amanda's arm and pulled her around to the other side of the car. "Tell him we finally have a caretaker who's a real self-starter. A guy who's on the spot without even being asked."

I opened the passenger door and helped Amanda inside. She smiled. She was clearly enjoying the situation. I went to the driver's side and stopped in front of Harmala. I stared into his dead eyes. I didn't intend to let him spoil something that had taken me years to build. Our faces were half a metre apart. I spoke quietly.

"You're not going to say anything to anybody. You don't want me to tell Henrik that there's something between you and his daughter that has you running after her and taking things out of her bag, for safe keeping. Do you want to show me what you took out of it a minute ago?"

116

He didn't say anything.

"Keep your mouth shut," I said calmly. "I'm driving Amanda home. That's all."

He raised his chin and lowered his eyelids. The intended effect was apparently to seem to be looking down on me. We stared at each other. Then we heard approaching footsteps and cheerful conversation. Harmala smiled that same smile that was no deeper than the surface.

"Good night to both of you," he said, and left without waiting for an answer.

Before the two men and two women approaching had reached us I turned the key in the ignition and drove away. I cursed myself. I'd wanted to be a hero, to stop a man from striking a woman, and what had I really done? I may have put everything in danger. And I'd strutted and threatened while I was at it. It was as if my former self had suddenly come back to life. Why had I got between the two of them and forgotten why I was there in the first place? But I knew the answer to that — she was sitting in the car beside me.

I glanced in the rearview mirror and caught a glimpse of Harmala's white shirt. It didn't look at all fancy any more.

The slam of the car door boomed over the cobblestone surface of Liisankatu. The sound bounced from wall to wall until it faded into the dark sky and the street had an unreal look in the light of the streetlamps, as if every stone were a different height and shape from every other. I stood on the pavement for a moment. I knew where Amanda lived. She'd told me. At the time, just a few nights ago, I hadn't thought that I'd soon have a use for the information. We hadn't talked in the car. Amanda had remained facing forward. The outline of her face and body had made me feel both heroic and extremely stupid.

I went around and opened the passenger door and held out her keys. She made no move to take them.

"You're not going to leave me in the street, are you?" she said.

There was no elevator. The sturdy stone steps of the old jugendstijl apartment house were low and wide, the kind that are as difficult as possible to climb. You don't know whether to take little steps or stretch out your stride to two at a time. I followed Amanda. I could smell her perfume, see the shape of her, the movements of her legs and ass under her thin dress.

On the third floor she opened a door and looked me in the eye.

"Now that you've rescued me, what do you want to do?"

I walked inside and switched on the light. Amanda followed. I heard the door close.

"I'm going in here," she said, stepping into a bathroom off the hallway. The stylish old white-painted wooden door closed silently.

I looked around.

There was a tall mirror in a brown wooden frame on one wall of the hall and a coat rack covered in clothes on the other. A shoe rack with about twenty pairs of shoes.

118

The living room was rectangular with three windows facing the street on one long wall. The original wood floor was beautifully finished and in excellent condition. To the right was a wide entrance to a bedroom and next to it a pale green ceramic stove. In the middle of the room was a steel table with a glass top, behind it a sleek, soft, white sofa flanked by two matching armchairs.

The other furniture — a steel floor lamp arching like a tsunami from behind the sofa, a dark, straight line of shelf for the designer Danish television, the vases on the windowsill, the square, black dish in the centre of the sofa table — all looked carefully considered. And of course stylish, expensive, and joyless. There was a kitchen and a small office to the left.

The Italian kitchen was gleaming and hygienic. I turned on the tap, which was of a presumably carefully chosen minimalist design. I got a glass from the cupboard and filled it. The kitchen was the size of my apartment. In the middle of the room was a long, black dining table like a fresh asphalt road. Around it were eight steel-legged chairs with black backs like giant flyswatters. The two lamps with metal hoods that hung over the table felt too bright. I turned them off. My eyes adjusted to the dark quickly, the meagre glimmer from the window on the far wall was enough to keep me from running into anything.

The window faced the building courtyard below. There was a light shining in the middle of it. It cast a hazy, feverish glow that was reflected yellow from the still-leafy shrubs and the red paving stones. I drank the water and knew I was in the wrong place, but sometimes, I told myself, you have to be in the wrong place in order to find the right one. I don't know if I believed myself.

"Just water?"

I turned.

Amanda was standing in the doorway with her right hand behind her back and her left hand rubbing her hair, then her nose.

"Nothing stronger?"

I shook my head. She pulled her hand from behind her back and stuffed something into her jeans pocket.

Neither of us said anything more. We were kissing. I took her completely into my arms, put my palms under her ass, and lifted her onto the edge of the table. I tore off her shirt, kissed her neck, tasted her skin. She pushed her chest against my face. I kissed her round breasts and then her hot, wet lips again. I took off my own shirt. I carried her to the bedroom, put her down on the bed, and pulled her jeans off. I left them where they fell, pushed her further onto the bed, and tugged off her black knickers. She spread her legs and pushed herself against my mouth. I licked for a moment, then rose and lowered myself onto her. We bit each other's lips. I looked into her eyes and saw a complete stranger. Our hips pounded together. The sweat was pouring off us. All the fury, fear, and jealousy I felt was in every thrust. Amanda scratched my back, my shoulders, panting. When I came, I heard her say something, but I couldn't hear what it was.

120

I lay on the bed. I heard the sound of the shower, stared at the ceiling. The sweat dried, leaving my skin leathery. The thought of the taste of her, how she felt under me, slippery and tight, made something in my lower abdomen tremble and my mouth turn dry. So fast, I thought. When I'd made love with Miia I'd been satisfied, calmed, for hours afterwards. Now the same restlessness that had made me clutch at Amanda, tear her clothes off and dive on top of her had immediately returned.

The bathroom door opened and Amanda came back into the room and stood naked at the end of the bed. She rubbed her nose, pulling the air into her nostrils like a boxer. It was hard to look at her without feeling an animal lust and a desire to possess her. Both feelings were the very thing that had always got me into difficulties.

"Caretaker," Amanda said, smiling as if she'd won something, "you seem to know what you want."

"I guess so."

"I think that's a good sign."

She lowered her knees to the bed and climbed over me on all fours. Up close, her eyes were shiny and hard and her gaze sharp. The inside of her thigh was soft against my leg.

"But you know what?" she said.

"What?"

"I'm going to go to sleep."

Her tone told me what she meant.

"I'll take a shower and go," I said.

"You've got potential," she said, pressing her lips against mine and kissing long and hot. Then she got up without looking at me, put on her robe, and went into the kitchen.

The neighbourhood was quiet and empty when I left on foot towards Saarinen's apartment in Eira, and my car. I walked across Senate Square, so deserted I could hear my own footsteps, the cathedral glowing white against the black night sky.

SEPTEMBER 2013

A few hours later an early Friday morning was dawning with its cloudless sky over the elegance of Eira when I saw Markus Harmala drive a black Lexus out from under a building onto the street. I'd been sitting in my Volvo a hundred metres away from the door to Saarinen's city apartment, trying to tame my thoughts.

Harmala was alone in the car. He looked both ways and put on his indicator. The car was turning in my direction. I lay down on my side and waited for him to pass. I sat up and looked in my wing mirror. The Lexus's indicator was still blinking. He was turning right.

I started the car, pressed in the clutch, and made a quick U-turn. I caught sight of the Lexus climbing Korkeavuorenkatu towards downtown, but kept my distance.

The Lexus crested the hill, then rolled sedately to the intersection at Esplanadi Park. Harmala slowed his speed and stopped the car halfway to the pedestrian crossing, then turned on his hazard lights and opened the driver's door. I turned right and went back up the hill and around the block, and parked as close as I could on the adjoining street. I couldn't see the Lexus, but I assumed it was still parked in the same spot. I waited. Then I felt a twinge of doubt.

I got out of the car, walked to the end of the block, and peered around the corner. Yes, the Lexus was still there, its hazards still blinking, but Harmala was standing in the street smoking a cigarette, looking as if he was waiting for someone. I went back to my car. The stone building where the Lexus was parked was where Henrik Saarinen kept a second-floor office.

I felt the sleepless night through my whole body. My legs ached, my eyes stung. I took hold of the steering wheel and squeezed. I had to be careful not to lean back against the seat. That would have made me fall asleep.

Finally the Lexus slipped past in front of me. Someone was sitting in the back seat. I would have recognised Saarinen — this was someone else. Harmala circled the Havis Amanda statue and soon we were both driving along the North Shore Road. The eastern horizon was a gentle pink, unbroken by clouds. The sea was a dark carpet, the islands were holes cut in it. The modern high-rises at Merihaka stood like giant toy blocks left behind on their lonely outcropping.

Keeping a safe distance from the Lexus was as hard as I remembered. Following one car in another isn't like in the movies. Not even remotely. I'd learned that years ago trying to stay behind Saarinen on his night outings. The world had never seemed so filled with traffic lights, pedestrians, lane changes, visual obstructions, sudden stops, unexpected turns, rocketing accelerations, and daredevil passes as when I absolutely had to keep a steady, uninterrupted speed.

The Lexus pulled onto the freeway. I let a city bus pull out from the stop in front of me. It served as a screen as we crossed over Kulosaari bridge. The landscape opened up. The sea was on both sides, the pure morning light all around us. For a few seconds I had a feeling of lightness, as if moving of my own volition, going somewhere that I wanted to go. The feeling faded quickly as the bus in front of me pulled over at another stop and I saw the black car some hundred metres ahead.

We passed three metro stations and the Lexus signalled to exit at Itäkeskus shopping centre. We drove straight until the road pulled a trick and veered left without changing its name.

We drove into an upmarket neighbourhood. The streets narrowed, the houses grew larger. It was still early and there was no traffic, so I gave the Lexus plenty of room. I nearly drove past the turn, took a right and slowed to a crawl, pulling over as soon as I spotted them.

They had stopped in front of a large white house. Harmala was slamming the back door of the car. A garage door on the street level of the three-storey building was just lowering. The passenger had gone inside. Harmala opened the driver's door.

He stood where he was for a moment, reached in his pocket, and lit a cigarette. He was facing the sea. The smoke from his cigarette was dark blue in the bright morning air.

The house was new, rising up like a just-opened gift from the god of Mammon. Half of the wall facing the street was glass. You could probably see the Baltic from the top floor. I wondered how much a plot in this area cost. Maybe half a million. The house itself a couple of million. Whoever built it would hardly have needed a loan for the project.

Who lived here? I typed the address into my phone's memory. The car had come from Henrik Saarinen's office, but the passenger wasn't Henrik Saarinen. Maybe it didn't matter who was in the car. I was more interested in Harmala's movements.

He finished smoking his cigarette, dropped the butt on the driveway, rubbed the sole of his shoe over it, and looked out in the direction of the rising sun. Then he got in the car and drove away.

The Lexus disappeared around a bend before I could turn the key and shift into gear. I kept my distance as we crossed over the freeway and turned left. It was easier to follow him now that there was more traffic. We reached an industrial area with three cars between us. We took another left, then right. I was in no hurry. I saw the Lexus turn right again and disappear around a corner, behind a building. I came to the intersection and slowed down. If the Lexus was parked on the road I would drive past it and come back from a different direction.

The road opened in front of me, straight and empty. It was lined with industrial buildings fronted by gates broad enough for large lorries. I looked into the building yards as I passed and came to the end of the road without seeing the Lexus.

I was about to make a U-turn when my phone rang. I pulled over. Unknown number. I answered with my name.

"Henrik Saarinen here. Good morning."

I looked at the clock on the dash — 7.15.

"Good morning."

"I see I didn't wake you."

"Not at all."

"I remember your application mentioned a driving licence. That you have one."

"Yes."

"Well, it just so happens that my driver has the day off and I need someone to do some driving. I have my car here in Helsinki. If you leave Kalmela now you could be here by nine."

My eyes had wandered to a sign that said we were in Roihupelto.

"Yes."

"Yes, you'll be here by nine, or yes, such a thing is theoretically possible?"

"I'll be there by nine," I said.

"Thanks. I won't call again."

He hung up. I thought for a moment. Was this a coincidence? The timing was amazing.

My plan had been to use Markus Harmala to get closer to Henrik Saarinen. That was why I'd followed him here. And now Saarinen was asking me to come to his house.

With morning traffic it would take half an hour to drive from East Helsinki to Eira. So I still had an hour. I pulled out again; I wanted to try one more time to find the Lexus. The more I knew about Harmala the better.

In addition to gates, some of the nearby buildings had ramps leading to lower level entrances. I was nearly back to the end of the street when I got a bite. I passed a ramp and thought I could see the shining back end of the Lexus in its depths. I parked the Volvo on the street fifty metres away and got out of the car.

It was a three-storey building that looked as if it was built in the 1980s, judging by its crumbling windowsills, the pale concrete used for the structure and surface, darkened in places, and its general boxiness. The poor construction showed in the ever so slight slant of the walls. The front of the building was unkempt, the strip of muddy, greyish lawn half filled with old appliances. The corpses of a refrigerator, washing machine, and microwave oven seemed to still cling to a hope of something better. Between them were boxes full of old hoses and cords. From the looks of them, the boxes had been outdoors for a number of winters.

The ramp led steeply into the building interior. I waited a moment, looking and listening. I didn't see anyone on the street, and a quick glance showed no one in the windows. I walked down the ramp and was surprised how dark and cold it was under the building. I felt as if I'd stepped into a cave. I let my eyes adjust to the sudden darkness. I didn't want to stand in silhouette against the bright morning, so I moved closer to the wall. After a while I thought I could make out the shapes of several vehicles. I didn't hear any sounds of cars or people. I could smell petrol and some other sharp, industrial smell. I was annoyed at how slowly my eyes adjusted to the dark. Finally I was able to see better. I had been right that the shapes were cars, but I hadn't realised that they really were only shapes. Many of them were at least partially disassembled. Harmala's Lexus was easy to pick out from the group. It was the only entire car in the garage.

I could see a grey steel door at the back of the space, partially opened. I headed towards it, and soon heard Harmala's voice through the crack. He sounded upset. I made my way closer, keeping near the wall. To get to the door I had to squeeze between two car bodies. It was a tight space and there were car parts strewn all over the floor, so I had to watch my feet, just when I should have been looking ahead.

The steel pipe struck me in the diaphragm. The blow was a powerful one, and I immediately doubled over. The pain spread inward and I couldn't get any air.

In front of me was a pair of distressed jeans tucked into combat boots. I lunged at them.

I couldn't quite reach the legs. They dodged out of my way. The second blow of the pipe struck me on my right arm, which I'd lifted to protect my head. I turned and lunged again.

This time I didn't miss. I was bent over facing the ground but I managed to wrap my arm around the pipe-wielder's waist. I'd moved with enough force to drive both of us against the junked car. The crash sounded like a bomb going off in the low-ceilinged room. I let go and rolled to the side.

The pipe was on the floor.

I grabbed it with both hands and swung it with all my strength in the direction of my attacker, and thought I grazed someone's side or back. I heard a cry and another crash against the side of the car.

In the same motion I got up from the floor and took off at a run towards the light. The blow to my gut had made my eyes water. I couldn't get a breath. I came to the ramp, pushed myself up and out of the building in two running strides, and rolled away from the entrance and out of view.

I stood up on the lawn and ran as hard as I could with a nearly ruptured diaphragm and no oxygen. I reached my car, which I'd left on the street in front of a blue-sided delivery van. The van served as a screen.

I threw myself behind the wheel, started the car, and drove away. The seatbelt reminder beeped for a couple of blocks before I was able to raise my right hand high enough to fasten it. I came to the traffic light and panted, bent over the steering wheel. Only then did I start to really feel the pain in my arm. The blow had struck me under the elbow and the pain buzzed in both directions. My fingers were stiff, partially numb. I couldn't touch my abdomen. I heard a car horn behind me. I realised the light was green and I hadn't moved. My eyes were dim. It was hard to breathe. I drove over the bridge past the Siilitie metro station and continued

130

toward Viikki. I looked in the rearview — no one was following me.

The straight section nearly a kilometre long between open fields proved challenging. I didn't want to attract attention so I made myself drive at the speed limit, which felt too fast. I held my right arm against my side. I sat upright, my back as straight as I could make it, though my solar plexus and stomach wanted me to put my head down on the steering wheel. I came to a roundabout.

I went nearly all the way around it, drove into the Viikki test gardens, found a car park, and a space at the far edge to pull into. I went to sit in the shade of the autumn trees, looked at the gold-brown leaves and felt the cold stone beneath me. I checked the clock on my mobile phone.

Still a few minutes.

A little bird flew among the branches in a precise trajectory, without hesitation, without a single unnecessary movement of its wings.

A moment later I was driving towards Eira.

Henrik Saarinen was nowhere to be seen. That was a good thing, and to be expected — it was only ten to nine. I could stroll up and down the pavement and shake out my arm and let the Disprin take effect. I'd stopped at a chemist's to buy some painkillers and swallowed two tablets on the spot, washing them down with cold, fresh water from the dispenser. Four cups. I was thirsty.

The wind blew such a strong smell of the sea that you'd have thought the middle of the ocean was right around the next corner. It was actually half a kilometre to the shore. The sparse leaves on the trees rustled and clicked in the morning wind like cut paper. The blanket of autumn was spread over everything.

The feeling had returned to my arm and the pain in my abdomen was lessening. I walked back to the building.

Henrik Saarinen opened the door at exactly nine o'clock.

"The car's in the basement," he said.

The red carpet in the stairwell was soft as fresh-cut grass under my feet. We walked in complete silence. We came to the basement door. Saarinen opened it with a key and let me through. I went down the stairs. I could hear Saarinen's feet on the stone steps and feel him behind me, his presence, which was so familiar to me now that its nearness felt both suffocating and oddly natural at the same time. I came to a low, grey fire door, pushed it open, and smelled a garage, a smell that's always and everywhere the same. The combination of rubber, petrol, dirty metal and stale air was the same whether you were in Kuala Lumpur, San Francisco, or an upmarket residential area in Helsinki. I was heading automatically towards the grey Mercedes-Benz at the back of the garage when I heard Saarinen speak.

"The Land Cruiser."

There were around sixteen parking spaces in the garage. A steel-grey Land Cruiser was parked in the middle on the right.

"You drive," Saarinen said.

I turned and caught the keys he tossed me. I found and pressed the button on the keychain to open the doors. The car lights flashed, the doors unlocked, and we got in. Saarinen sat next to me in the front seat. It wasn't enough that we were in a different car, he also wanted to sit in a different way from usual.

The Land Cruiser was nimbler than you would guess from its appearance. It turned in the tight space without a problem and bounded into the street like a smaller, low-slung car.

"Head toward Kalmela," Saarinen said.

"All right," I said, and turned left towards the shore road.

I tried to watch him from the corner of my eye. His face didn't tell me anything, he gazed straight ahead. He was dressed in a way that was no doubt as ordinary as he could manage. Light blue jeans, a red sweatshirt, and a black training jacket. His shoes were a different matter — they looked like tough safety shoes, with thick soles and steel reinforcements; the kind of shoes construction workers wear.

"So you didn't have any problem getting here," Saarinen said as we came to the tree-lined end of Mechelinkatu.

"No trouble," I answered. "Harmala's day off must have been a surprise, then?"

"Yes and no. The way surprises sometimes happen. A surprise I had expected."

We passed the hospital. The traffic lights were green as we rolled down the hill, turned onto the highway, and accelerated to a hundred kilometres per hour.

"I'm not certain of the exit, so be ready to turn when I tell you to," he said.

"Got it."

I could feel him looking at me.

"You haven't asked anything," he said.

"What should I ask?"

"That depends on what you want to know. To be honest, you look like a man who doesn't really have any questions. A person like that is always interesting. It's either due to a complete lack of interest, or to the fact that you already know what you want to know. I'll bet that in this case it's the latter."

"True. For your needs, anyway. I have the car keys, and clear directions."

I glanced at Saarinen. He had a tight little smile on his face. He was a large man. His face was about ten centimetres above mine.

"Fantastic," he said. "Just fantastic. Better than I expected. We're going to have a wonderful day."

I didn't ask what he meant, and he didn't say anything more. He didn't speak again until we were in Espoo.

"Turn here," he said, pointing at an exit.

I drove to the intersection and chose the direction and lane according to his instructions. When I saw a large lit sign I knew instinctively that we would end up under it. Saarinen gave single-word directions — *left, right, straight, park* — until we were in the car park of a large hardware store. I turned off the engine. Saarinen took something out of his pocket and handed it to me. A folded piece of paper.

134

"Shopping list," he said.

He didn't look as if he was planning to go in the store. Or anywhere. His eyes behind his glasses were serious.

"Evidently you want me to go in alone," I said.

"Yes, please."

I looked at him for a moment. Then I got out of the car and headed for the store entrance. I didn't look behind me. When I got inside, I unfolded the list:

50 metres 5mm rope
garbage bags (3 rolls)
steel shovels with pointed tips (2)
light chainsaw
hunting knives (2)
nail gun, 30° Paslode IM350+ (with storage case)
compressed air (4 cartridges)
90mm nails (to fit the nail gun — 10 packs of 53)
protective gloves (5 pairs)
protective goggles (2 pairs)

I got one of the large, blue shopping carts and gathered the items, walking at a steady pace down the long aisles of the warehouse. There weren't many customers, and I made quick progress. I'd found everything in fifteen minutes. I paid with the credit card he'd given me, and rolled the cart out to the car. Saarinen was sitting motionless in the front seat.

"Marvellous," he said when I'd put everything in the car and was once again behind the wheel.

I assumed that we would head to Kalmela now. When I approached the highway again I looked both ways and noticed a slight smile on Saarinen's lips, a kind of smile I hadn't seen on him before. It made something scratch at me from inside, made the gall rise to the back of my throat, sent a cold wind blowing through me.

I looked straight ahead again and let my foot fall on the accelerator with its full weight. The Land Cruiser leapt forward. Saarinen's neck jerked and his head rocked backwards, the smile disappearing from his suntanned face.

Bright sunlight bounced off the bonnet and wing mirror into my eyes. The landscape changed yet remained the same: autumn colours at their most red, yellow, and gold. I kept my eyes on the road and the traffic, in spite of my awareness that Saarinen's head was making tiny sideways movements as he glanced in my direction at regular intervals, nonchalantly.

After fifteen minutes of silence he opened his mouth. He didn't look at me as he spoke. Quite the opposite. He behaved as if he were counting the trees or watching the rise and fall of the cut rock that lined the right side of the road.

"Is it all right if we drop formalities and titles today?" he said, then answered himself. "Of course it is, since we're on unofficial business anyway."

I didn't know what about our business was particularly unofficial, but I wasn't going to ask, either.

136

"Do you remember when I asked about your family?"

I remember very well, I thought, because I was afraid I was being exposed.

But I just said, "I remember."

"How does it feel?"

"How does what feel?"

"Being alone in the world. Not having anyone who needs to be notified if anything happens to you. I don't mean to pry. You don't have to answer."

"I don't know," I said. "You can get used to anything."

"I thought you would say that. In those very words. So I don't believe you. Or I only partially believe you."

I held the steering wheel tightly and moved into the left lane to pass a tall, white bus, which seemed to grow longer as we came abreast of it.

"I'm sure you can get used to anything," Saarinen said. His voice was clear, without emotion, the words precise. "But that's not the whole truth. I assume I can be direct with you?"

I shrugged my shoulders. My back was wet with sweat. My heart pounded in my chest as if in an empty box, hollow and aching. Until now I'd thought I could maintain my composure and certainty, but the situation was becoming more uncomfortable by the second, and I wasn't sure why. Of course being near someone whom you suspect of murdering your mother is stressful, but there was something else, too.

"It must be very liberating in some ways," he said, still not looking at me but straight ahead, maybe at the old blue Saab in front of us. "Liberating in the sense that you can do as you see fit. You don't owe anything to anyone, and you won't be judged no matter what you do. You can behave as if you know what's best. You can take things on and get them done. Set goals and commit to them and not care about anything else, or anyone else, just about getting results."

My mind turned cooler than the air conditioning. Saarinen's hands lay in his lap, palms up. He opened and closed them as if calling down rain from the sky.

"When I look at you, Aleksi, it seems to me that you have a job to do. I'm rarely wrong about these things. I trust my instinct. I've used it to make quite a bit of money. And to do everything else. As you know."

Breathing was getting harder. My dry throat needed me to swallow, but made it difficult.

"I mean things like acquiring Kalmela. Some people might have thought the old house and grounds would be nothing but a burden, but I saw it as a possibility, a way to have something whose value would only increase as the years went by. That's what I mean about you. Don't think that I see you as nothing but a caretaker, a maintenance man."

As he spoke he turned his head like a machine, precise as a clock, level and sure. I looked at him. Our eyes met. I turned my gaze back to the road, his glistening eyes were oppressive.

"I see potential," he said. "Possibilities. Maybe something that even you aren't aware of. Do you think I'm going too far? That I'm jumping to unfounded conclusions?"

138

I shrugged again.

"Of course not. Of course not. I'm not mistaken. I'm sure that you're capable of anything," Saarinen said, no longer looking at me. "The question is, are you ready for anything?"

That's an easy question, I thought, as long as I don't have to explain my answer.

"Yes," I said.

"That's what I thought," he said with satisfaction. "That's why I brought you along today. And to get to know each other better, of course."

Having said this, he fell silent. Neither of us said anything for several minutes. I thought of turning on the radio, to hear the sounds of the outside world, other people's voices. Anything. I settled for silence.

"Naturally I have to ask you about some things that might seem personal," Saarinen said, as if there had been no break in his talk. "And of course you in turn can ask me questions."

Where did you bury my mother?

It wasn't yet time for that question. I wanted to get closer, to know more about him.

"We've got twenty minutes," I said.

Saarinen was quiet for a moment, then said, "What do you remember about your father, Aleksi?"

I was about to open my mouth when he answered his own question.

"Not very much. Otherwise you would have mentioned him in your interview. Don't be alarmed if I know everything that was asked in your interview, and all of your answers. It's all confidential."

"I promise not to be alarmed," I said.

"You have a sense of humour, too. That's wonderful. I remember my own father all too well. I don't know whether to hate him or thank him. I hope this isn't getting too personal."

"Not at all," I said.

I've worked for twelve years to get to this place.

"My father was a man who was never satisfied with anything." He sighed. "That dissatisfaction applied to me, as well. It made me try harder. Not that trying did any good. I don't remember him ever giving me a word of praise for anything or ever showing me any recognition. Which in hindsight is actually the secret of my success."

I waited for him to continue. I glanced sideways, straight into his eyes.

"I hate him, and I'm grateful to him," he said. "I wasn't truly free until after he died."

I looked at the road again. We passed the kilometre mark. We would soon turn in at the estate. Or not.

"When did your father die?" I asked.

"May the fourth, 1983."

"Then what happened?"

"What do you mean?"

"You said you were really free after he died. What exactly was this freedom?"

"And you're just a maintenance man. Is that right?"

I glanced at him again. He had the same thin little smile on his face as he had had when we'd left the hardware store. Thin, and rotten through.

140

I flipped on the indicator and flowed into the exit lane that arched gently down to the right. Saarinen didn't say anything, from which I assumed we were still going to the estate. I could see in the rearview mirror that we were the only vehicle exiting. As if everyone else knew of a better place to go. When we pulled onto the highway I accelerated and felt as alone as Saarinen had just guessed I was. He broke the silence.

"You have an excellent grasp of things. Just think of the places we'll go once we start to discuss our shared future."

SEPTEMBER 1993

Well, what do you want to be? my mother asks as we sit down to eat. Meat sauce is steaming in the cast-iron skillet and next to it is a pot of spaghetti with a ladle standing in it. Through the rising steam she looks as if she's sitting in a fog across from me. She smiles expectantly.

My teacher's question has been bothering me, for many reasons. I listened in embarrassment to the answers of the other thirteen-year-olds and felt taken by surprise. Like an outsider. It wasn't my classmates' answers that caught me off guard, it was that they had an answer, their certainty on the subject. Policeman, doctor, singer, gamekeeper, baker. I've simply never thought that I ought to want to be something, to know what awaits me. I also noticed that many of the boys' answers were their fathers' professions.

Help yourself while you think about it, my mother says.

No. I'm not hungry.

Are you feeling bad?

No.

You'll feel better if you eat something.

I sigh as audibly as possible and take hold of the ladle. I put some spaghetti on my plate and ladle on the sauce. My favourite meal. I sprinkle some cheese on top and watch as my mother fills her plate.

Why don't we know anything? I ask.

Oh, honey, she says. Just eat.

I pick up my fork. It doesn't seem connected to the food on my plate at all. I ask again.

Why can't we at least know what kind of work he did?

She stops eating.

That has nothing to do with anything. You can be whatever you plan to be. That's what the question is about. It's about your plans. But everything will change along the way. Life is like that. You start from one place, and it leads you to another place, and that takes you to another. It's very unusual to know when you're thirteen what you're going to be doing twenty or thirty years from now.

Everybody else knows.

They don't really know. They just say what their mothers —

And their fathers, I add. That's the thing.

She looks at me a moment longer and then continues eating. The kitchen window is open. I can hear familiar voices from the courtyard below. Boys and girls who don't eat with their families at home, who never have regular, scheduled meals, are playing in the yard. My mother is strict about those things. We always eat the way we're eating now.

Do you feel bad about it? she asks.

I can see in her eyes that this is hard for her, too. She's not eating her dinner. She has her hair tucked behind her ears, she's wearing a green hooded sweatshirt, and at that moment she looks ten years younger than she is.

Sometimes, I say.

It doesn't matter what your mother or father's profession is. It just doesn't. You'll see.

She gets herself another twist of spaghetti and ladles sauce on top of it, more quickly than before.

Well, what was it? I ask.

What was what?

His profession? What did he do?

We've talked about this many times.

You never answer me.

Not everything has an answer.

I drop my fork onto my plate with a clank and put my elbows on the table. I realise that soon I'll be bigger than my mother. She seems to have shrunk over the course of this conversation.

Maybe not everything has an answer, I say. But this does.

I look her in the eye, as sincerely as I know how. A shadow flashes over her face, although the daylight is still coming through the window behind me and brightening her eyes.

Sometimes the less you know, the better, she says in a soft voice. Besides, your father didn't really have a profession.

Was he unemployed?

Far from it, but not all work is the kind that you can name. If a person cuts hair, then he's a barber, but if he just thinks and watches what happens and makes decisions, it's harder to know what to call it.

You've never told me that my father thinks and watches. You've never told me what he did.

Well I'm telling you now, she says. And that's all I know. All I can know. Now let's eat.

She does what she says; she starts to eat. The long light of a summer evening suits her; she looks young and innocent. I feel as if I've been hit. As if there's a moat between me and the world, a fortress wall, and behind the wall there's an archer. It's all impossible. Then I realise something, with a clarity I've never felt before.

I know what I'm going to do when I grow up, I say.

My mother raises her head.

I'm going to look for answers.

Her expression changes. There's something in her face that I can't quite read.

SEPTEMBER 2013

It seemed it was just Henrik Saarinen and me at Kalmela. There were no cars in the drive or in the parking area behind the main house. Even Enni's Škoda was gone. Maybe today was some kind of general day off and they'd forgotten to tell me.

The adrenaline that had kept me awake and alert on the drive, and for hours before that, was starting to clear out of my system. I'd been awake for a day and a half, and every cell knew it. My eyes stung, and must have been red, my stomach was growling and I was weak from lack of food. I stood next to the car for a moment regaining my balance. The wind blew waves of sea scent. It felt right and good. I let it cool me from head to toe, and wasn't cold. The sun peeked out from between dark clouds, tenacious and bright, as I opened my coat and felt the little volume of poetry in my back pocket and remembered my mother's name written in it.

"We can leave these things in the car," Saarinen said, slamming the passenger door.

When I didn't follow him, he stopped and turned around.

"What is it?"

"Nothing," I said. "It's nice to get a breath of fresh air."

Saarinen looked around.

"Quiet. Splendidly quiet."

Having said this he turned softly again and started walking towards the main house. A large man against a large sea, forest, and sky. Thick, strong arms hanging at his sides like the stout ropes of a seagoing ship, ready for any storm. I shook the fatigue from my head once again and took the first step. I heard the phone ring in my pocket and saw Saarinen stop again, hesitating.

"Go ahead and answer it," he said. "There's no hurry."

I pulled the phone from my pocket.

Amanda.

Her first question was, "Is this a bad time to call?"

"Not at all," I said.

I gestured to Saarinen that he could go on without me with whatever he was doing. He surprised me by obeying and continuing to the house. I took a few steps in the opposite direction so that my voice wouldn't reach him.

"Can I ask you something?" Amanda said.

"Of course."

"How did you end up there?"

"Where?"

"Eira, last night."

"Just a coincidence."

"A coincidence?"

"I had to go to Helsinki. I had some business in town."

That was true. So why did I sound so defensive?

"That makes three of us, then," Amanda said. "Three people who just happened to stumble onto the same street corner in the middle of the night."

"Yeah," I said, wondering where the conversation was going.

"Did you hear what Harmala and I were talking about?"

I actually hadn't heard a word of it. Amanda interpreted my silence to mean the opposite.

"It wasn't what you think. I just wanted to tell you that."

"What do you mean?" I said. "I didn't hear anything."

I didn't want to hear about Amanda and Harmala's relationship. Or I did, but this wasn't the time.

"I can't figure you out, caretaker. Can I trust you?"

"Of course," I said, looking over the water to the horizon. The sea was blue and level.

"Where are you?" she asked suddenly, in a completely different tone of voice, light and carefree. Henrik Saarinen was just a little doll in the distance now.

"At Kalmela," I said.

"So last night you were here and now you're there. You know who you remind me of? My father. He's up all night and then he's as perky as ever, even if he didn't sleep at all."

Saarinen disappeared behind the house.

"Does he do that?" I said.

"He always has. He says he can sleep when he's dead."

"He's here," I said.

"My father?"

"Yeah."

She didn't say anything for a second.

"That's nice. You can get to know each other. If he can learn to trust you, like I have. You might get within striking distance, as they say."

I tried to gauge how ironically she meant this, but my thoughts were interrupted when Saarinen came out from behind the house. The distance between us was about a hundred metres. He walked to an open spot and waved to me with his right hand, beckoning. As if that and the phone call weren't enough, a familiar car pulled into the drive.

"Amanda, let's talk a little later," I said, and hung up.

Ketomaa stopped his old Citroën Xantia, on its last legs, and remained sitting in the car. I didn't move either. Saarinen stopped at the corner of the house and dropped his bag beside him. We formed a nearly equilateral triangle, an arrangement that felt contrived, like a scene in an old western. And it was contrived, of course, at least in the sense that Ketomaa couldn't have been there by accident. I walked towards his car. Saarinen did the same a second later. I couldn't see whether he'd paused to watch me or made the decision on his own.

Ketomaa got out of the car. Saarinen and I approached from two directions. Ketomaa didn't look at either of us, keeping his eyes focused in front of him, between the two of us. As I got closer I saw him squint. Closer still and I saw that he was blinded, having just removed his sunglasses. He had painful-looking, purplish indentations on either side of his long, pale nose, distillations of the essence of his thin presence. His grey suit was both old and grown too large for him. The collar of his white shirt was yellowed and his blue necktie was neatly knotted but ready to fray. It was as if both the man and everything he was wearing might go to pieces at any moment.

I knew Ketomaa and I knew that it was all a bluff. It was an impression he wanted to give: a wrinkled old man, forgetful of his appearance. So I wasn't surprised when he offered me his hand and introduced himself audibly.

"Ketomaa. Good day."

Saarinen came to where we were standing. I didn't give him a glance, looked into Ketomaa's eyes. They didn't tell me anything. It was like looking at sky or water, his eyes were just there.

"Aleksi Kivi," I said, letting go of his hand and stepping to the side.

Saarinen thrust out a large, eager hand.

"Henrik Saarinen. I'm glad you were able to come."

Ketomaa and Saarinen shook hands. I knew without looking that the grip was firm on both sides. Ketomaa had a small, agreeable smile on his lips.

"It's a wonderful spot," he said.

"Thank you. It's my pride and joy. That's why you're here." Saarinen turned towards me.

Ketomaa had to make a half turn to face me. I stood without saying a word. I was careful to keep my expression calm and relaxed. What was happening behind my eyes and between my ears was another matter. My pulse was racing and I was afraid the throb of the veins on my neck was about as inconspicuous as a dog's wagging tail. I could hear my own blood churning in my ears and I thought my weary, hungry, beaten body might fail me at any moment. The wind off the water ruffled my hair but I didn't feel cooled in the least.

"Aleksi, I'm sure you don't mind if we finish a little later. I need to go inside and chat with Mr Ketomaa for a moment."

"Of course," I said. "I'll get the things out of the car. Just tell me where to put them."

Saarinen looked at me and smiled.

"Don't bother. I want to keep them in the car. You can focus on your own job, your own work."

"And what is your job?" Ketomaa asked.

I looked at him.

"Caretaker," I said. "I'm the caretaker."

"Be forewarned that this man is a private investigator," Saarinen said with a smile. It was a contemptuous, self-satisfied smile not very different from the grin I'd seen several times already that morning. "He won't rule anyone out as a suspect."

Having said this, he turned to Ketomaa.

"Although as far as I can tell Aleksi is entirely trustworthy. I'm rarely wrong about these things. In fact I have the impression that Aleksi is one of the most straightforward men I've ever met."

They were both looking at me now. I felt them studying my face, watching for my reaction. I knew I looked tired, but how tired? I didn't say anything. I hoped the ground would stay firmly under my feet, both figuratively and literally.

"Are you trustworthy?" Ketomaa asked.

"Of course," I said. "One hundred per cent."

"And you're not mixed up in any way in what I've come to investigate?"

It was Saarinen's turn to interject. "Aleksi doesn't know anything about it. He doesn't need to."

Ketomaa kept his eyes on me. I had no idea what they were talking about. It felt like a nightmare, a bad dream where you can't run or move your limbs no matter how hard you try.

"About what?" I asked.

"Even in a beautiful place like this ugly things sometimes happen," Saarinen said. "We can talk about it later."

"Talk about what?" I said, aiming my question at Ketomaa this time. Not that I expected him to answer. I just wanted to hear him talk.

"I'm bound to strict confidentiality. But the two of you will have a chance to talk later."

His face was as solemn as the grave. He seemed to mean every word he said. Even Saarinen stopped smiling.

"We should be going. Please follow me."

Ketomaa looked at me one more time. I still couldn't read anything in his eyes or his face. He turned. He was so thin and his suit coat was so large that the turn seemed to occur in two movements, first the man inside the coat, then the broad shoulders of his jacket.

I watched them disappear into the house. The large black doorway swallowed them quickly and easily.

I knew that I had to get something to eat and lie down. I headed inside, to my own small apartment above the storage shed. I climbed the stairs and opened the door, which was unlocked. The rooms were as quiet as a mouse. I made a sandwich and sat by the window to eat it. The soft oat bread, pepperoni, and melted cheese tasted delicious and set off my dormant hunger. I trotted back and forth between the kitchen and the table making more sandwiches and eating them. After the sixth one I made some coffee and drank it while it was too hot, burning my tongue and my throat.

I thought I would be too tired to think, but I wasn't. Everything that had happened revolved in my mind in confused fragments that I tried to make sense of. Ketomaa was here. That alone stoked a thousand separate fears. Fear that Ketomaa would reveal who I was and tell Saarinen what I was doing there. How had Ketomaa turned up right here, right now? He was here in a private investigator's capacity, that was clear. But why? If Saarinen wanted to hire a detective, how was it that the one he hired happened to be Ketomaa? And what was it he was here to investigate?

I was completely spent. I hurt all over.

My biggest question was this: had I lost the only person I had from the past, the only person I could trust? Was I as alone in the world as I sometimes felt I was?

I leaned my right elbow on the table and tried to keep my eye on the Citroën in the yard. Falling asleep seemed like an impossibility, but my body knew better. It knew more than I did.

There was a short series of three knocks on the door, each one progressively louder. The last one could have been heard all the way to Helsinki. I instinctively looked out of the window. Ketomaa's car was still outside. I got up and almost fell over. The pain was suddenly awakened, my gut and side reminding me of the beating I'd taken. I held onto the wall for support and looked at the clock. I'd slept on my right arm for an hour and a half and it was completely numb. I jiggled my shoulder and opened the door.

"There's been a change of plans," Saarinen said. "We can do it later. I have to go to Helsinki."

I'd just woken up and probably looked like it. Saarinen's eyes were covered by large, black sunglasses.

"You look like you've had a shock," he said. "Has something happened?"

The question sounded empathetic, but there was a trace of a smile at the corner of his mouth that didn't express fellow-feeling.

"No. I think I dozed off. What plans do you mean?"

"We were supposed to spend the day together, remember? But I have to return to Helsinki right away."

"What's happened?"

Saarinen didn't answer immediately.

"Nothing that affects our work."

"Our work?"

"As I said this morning, I see you as something more than a handyman. We need to discuss your job duties later. And other things, too, of course. But right now I have errands waiting for me. I have to go."

I remembered something.

"Those things are still in the car."

"Of course they are," he said, smiling again. "That's fine. And the car's staying here. I'm getting a lift into town with Ketomaa."

I was finally completely awake.

"The private eye?"

The black sunglasses hid his expression, the changes in his face, what his words really meant, what was left unsaid. I felt like tearing them off his face so I could see the truth.

"Yes. Why does that surprise you?"

Which of us was pretending the most? Which one knew that the other one knew that he knew something the other one didn't know?

"I was just thinking about our errand this morning. And the car. That's all."

"All in good time," Saarinen said. "And that time is still to come. And it shouldn't matter to you. You work for me. If I say you have the rest of the day off, then you have the rest of the day off."

"Of course."

"That's what power is. That's something else we'll talk more about later. Enjoy the afternoon."

He turned. His soft, quick movement was familiar to me. It still chilled me. I stood in the doorway and watched him as he went down three steps, stopped, turned again. The sunglasses reflected the brightness around him and made him a peculiar mixture of face and landscape.

"Why does Ketomaa provoke these emotions in you?"

"Emotions?"

"Insecure, awkward. Is it him, or the type of person he represents?"

"I didn't notice feeling insecure . . ."

"I noticed. I notice things like that. Ketomaa is well-known to me. Don't worry. He's under our control now."

The black sunglasses looked in my direction a moment longer, then Saarinen went down the stairs and disappeared around the corner of the house.

I closed the door and went to the window. Ketomaa walked to his car and stood with his back to me. His neck was thinner, the skin even paler than the last time I'd seen him. Henrik Saarinen folded himself into the car; Ketomaa stood beside it for a second. He turned his head only slightly, but it was enough. I knew that he knew I was watching him. A moment later he had lowered himself into the driver's seat, the Citroën started up, and he drove away.

I didn't have many options. I could demand an accounting of everything that was unclear to me, unjust, wrong, but there was no one who was the slightest bit obligated to tell me anything. Losing my self-control, surrendering my power to the undirected rage boiling inside me would spoil my chances. It would destroy my opportunity to find out the one thing I came here to find out.

I took a breath and decided to fall back on the tactic that had got me this far — my patience, my ability to wait for the right moment. It didn't just feel right, it also gave me an idea that I instantly latched onto.

A young criminal investigator Ketomaa had mentioned in connection with Tanja Metsäpuro was called Sami Mansikka-aho. He wasn't quite my age, although it may have seemed that way from Ketomaa's point of view. Mansikka-aho was nine years older than me, with broad shoulders, dark, curly hair, sharp blue eyes, and a beard that may have been ironic or earnest. He got another cup of the Chinese restaurant's bitter, yellowish coffee that tasted strangely of tea before we'd even had a chance to settle in and drink the first one. He pumped the thermos pitcher with quick, impatient gestures, came back to the table, and looked me in the eye.

"I have to admit," he said. "I was a little surprised."

"My mother disappeared twenty years ago. You investigated Tanja Metsäpuro's murder ten years ago. In my opinion the two cases have a lot in common."

Mansikka-aho scratched his cheek with the same impatient hand he'd just used to get the coffee.

"I mean the pattern for today," he said. "You get in touch with me and tell me Ketomaa can vouch for you, you assure me that you're a smart, honest guy. Then you ask me not to say anything about it to Ketomaa. Not that Ketomaa and I see each other all that often. I haven't seen him since he retired . . . what was it? A year ago? Two?"

His eyes were red and shining as if he'd just rubbed them with an onion. My eyes were probably much the same. We were both obviously tired, having not slept for our own separate reasons.

It was afternoon and the lunch rush was just ending. I'd reached Mansikka-aho at his desk and tried to start a conversation on the phone, but when he heard why I was calling he said that it was something we should discuss in person. I'd come to Helsinki in Henrik Saarinen's Land Cruiser — against Saarinen's express directions.

"I know it sounds a little contradictory, but you know my background."

We were sitting in the last booth in the back. He sipped his coffee, his lips pursed on the edge of the cup, his slurp audible. Behind him was an almost empty room with windows onto a car park. The rear end of the grey Land Cruiser looked like a hearse waiting for someone to step into it.

"I know what there is to know," he said, putting his cup down on his saucer with a clink and pausing a moment before looking at me. "Ketomaa was the original investigator. Over the years you two apparently

158

met or at least talked, since you know about Tanja and you knew I was on the case."

"So you know that I know quite a lot. I wanted to hear more about Tanja Metsäpuro. Presently . . ."

"My first stiff. First murder case, I mean."

"I know."

He raised one eyebrow. "There's no new information about Tanja."

"But you had a suspect."

"I can't tell you about that. The police can't —"

"I know it was Henrik Saarinen."

He leaned back in his seat.

"If Ketomaa's been telling you these things it could be considered professional misconduct."

"He didn't have to tell me. Henrik Saarinen is responsible for my mother's disappearance."

Mansikka-aho's red eyes didn't blink, his expression didn't change in any way. But something — something careless and relaxed — disappeared from his demeanour, without altering his face or posture. The difference could only be seen in his red eyes, which now seemed to be aimed more directly at me.

"And who have you proffered this theory to?"

"No one," I said. "No one except you and Ketomaa before."

"Nobody else?"

"No. Why?"

Mansikka-aho didn't answer my question. Instead he asked me, "How did Ketomaa react to this suggestion?"

"He says that even when a shoe's the right size it could be the wrong style. That not all water is rain.

That you can throw a bullseye one day and miss the mark for the rest of your life. And other things like that. In a nutshell he says that just because something seems true doesn't mean it is true. How well do you know Ketomaa?"

"Not very well, but a bit," Mansikka-aho said, seeming to be saying something more. "A bit."

I'd barely tasted my so-called coffee. It was probably unfit to drink by now, a sour puddle in front of me. I pushed the cup and saucer aside and leaned my elbows on the table.

"What about lately?" I asked. "Are you still investigating Tanja's murder?"

He looked at me for a second. "Why not ask Ketomaa about it? If he told you confidential information before, why not now? As far as I know he's still doing some kind of PI gigs, even if he's mostly retired. Why not call him?"

I didn't answer right away. Mansikka-aho noticed.

"Why don't you?"

"Why don't I what?"

"Why don't you ask Ketomaa? Is he not as obsessive as he used to be about the case?"

"Ketomaa? He never was. Just the opposite. He always told me I was on the wrong trail."

Mansikka-aho looked at me as if I was raving mad.

"You're kidding, right? He didn't seem to do anything else just before he retired. Spent all his time on your mother and Tanja Metsäpuro. He even pestered me with questions about it now and then. I told him what I told you. There's no new information."

I was about to ask, What about Henrik Saarinen, but suddenly the whole situation felt wrong. The smell of the greasy food, the music that was either one endless song or the same short song over and over, the cop with bloodshot eyes like the warning lights on some indecipherable machine. I could see in his face that he knew he'd made a mistake, he'd said something that had the exact opposite effect from what he'd expected. What could make an experienced cop behave that way? The bright autumn day flooded over me and the thought of fresh air and open sky was suddenly insistent.

"I have to go," I said.

"Wait," Mansikka-aho said.

I remained seated.

"If you know something about Ketomaa, you should tell me," he said. "If he's still chasing after innocent people, he's got to stop. This is a serious matter."

The restaurant was suddenly quiet, as if it had been abandoned.

"I understand," Mansikka-aho said, in a voice that was considerably softer than the one he'd used a moment before. "You've been through a hellish experience. It could give a person all kinds of ideas, and if those ideas were stoked up by a slightly daft old retiree, it could lead to all kinds of misunderstandings."

"What do you mean, stoked up?"

He leaned forward.

"Ketomaa didn't retire. He was forced out. Think about it. It started a long time ago."

"What did?"

"His bizarre behaviour. Not long after your mother disappeared, I think. And that was a long time ago. Almost twenty years."

"What kind of bizarre behaviour?"

"I can't talk about it, but let's just say that it had to do with this same obsessive need to find connections between suspects and crimes where there were no connections."

I didn't say anything. I was starting to realise the extent of the error I'd just made. Fatigue and emotion and disappointment and doubt had all got the upper hand after all.

"Of course," I said. "I'll tell you right away if I hear from him. It all sounds very odd."

"And what you said a moment ago about a certain person," Mansikka-aho said. "This Mr Saarinen. It's best to forget about it. There's nothing to support it."

"No, of course."

He smiled. His red eyes lit up again.

"It was nice to meet you," he said. "I'm glad you got in touch with me. Otherwise I don't know what might have happened."

There was something repellent about the items in the back of the Land Cruiser. They were just tools, but it felt as if they had a purpose. Otherwise Saarinen wouldn't have bought them.

I'd made a mistake about Ketomaa. He'd been a step, or many steps, ahead of me the whole time. I took my phone out of my pocket, found his number, and

162

tried to call him. The call went to voicemail. I was just about to leave a message, but snapped the phone off.

I was crossing the bridge at Pasila. Itä-Pasila rose up in front of me like a poor man's sci-fi city. The train tracks headed north and south on either side of the bridge, some of them startlingly rusty in the sunlight, tarnished and forgotten. The shinier ones shot under the bridge towards the station that loomed to my left, looking like an East German swimming stadium, a shameful reminder of the 1980s and '90s habit of building things as grey and ugly as they could possibly be and expecting them to come into their own once they were built, the way the hundred-year-old stone buildings in the city had.

I turned onto Aleksis Kivi street. I knew where I was going. There was no need to call ahead and say I was coming. I passed the Kallio library and drove along the Sörnäinen shore road toward the quiet of Kruunuhaka.

Why had Ketomaa spent years making me think that I was on the wrong track, barking up the wrong tree, when all the while he himself was trying any way he could to solve my mother's disappearance and Tanja Metsäpuro's murder? He even got fired for it, if Mansikka-aho was to be believed.

I had to drive up and down Liisankatu before I found a place to park. The Land Cruiser needed such a lot of room that it made you wonder how anyone thought of it as a city car. I left the parking unpaid. Liisankatu in the daytime seemed broader, seemed to lead somewhere. It had looked different at night.

163

I rang the buzzer. I rang it again. I was looking at the names listed by the door and pondering my next move when I heard a lively bark behind me. A small white dog wanted to go inside. On the other end of its lead was a middle-aged woman in thick-framed glasses and an oversized parka. She didn't give me a second look as she opened the door with her key and left me to decide whether I should enter or remain outside. I followed her in and went to the second floor, where the small white dog barked again and led the woman to her door. I climbed up to the third floor and rang the bell.

Finally I heard steps on the other side of the door. Then they stopped.

The door remained shut.

SEPTEMBER 2013

The next morning I walked down to the beach. The sea lay calm and blue. Not a leaf was moving in the trees on the shore. The sky black with rain was just a memory, a puddle here and there and the damp fragrance of the forest all around. I put my toolbox on the sauna porch and breathed in deeply. I needed to breathe. I had my requisite tools. If anyone asked, I was still the caretaker, doing my job.

I hadn't been able to reach Ketomaa. Enni had come back early that morning; I could tell by the fresh tracks of her Škoda's tyres in the mud. I hadn't heard anything from Amanda, no explanation for not answering the door. That didn't stop me from thinking about her. I was reminded of her by the bucket at the foot of the steps, where she'd had her fish and her knife on that stormy night. My paranoia about the meeting with Mansikka-aho still simmered in the back of my mind.

I sat with my hands folded and prayed for patience, looking out at the water. I told myself many times that everything was fine, everything was going as planned. I was so absorbed in my own thoughts that I didn't notice the sound of footsteps until they reached the porch floorboards, and I realised I'd heard them from far off before they registered.

Tall boots, black and shiny clean. The camouflage trousers and dark-blue safari jacket were also clean, looked brand new. His whole outfit was crisp with newness. Another thing that was new was a detail that made me immediately uneasy. A white bandage was wrapped around the right hand. A thick one. The bandage reached from inside the coat sleeve halfway down the fingers, leaving the thumb and fingertips free. So the wound was on the knuckles, the palm, or the back of the hand. It looked serious, but it didn't seem to affect the broad smile on his face.

"Working hard, of course," Saarinen said. "I'm not surprised. The morning's well advanced."

I stood up. Saarinen took off his sunglasses.

"Good morning."

I moved to the middle of the porch. For some reason I expected Ketomaa to be a few steps behind him, but he was alone. Of course. The idea that Ketomaa would be with him was absurd, a product of my own imagination. Or was it?

"It looks as if it rained all day and night. Or did it only start in the evening?"

"I didn't notice. It did rain hard during the night."

"Did it wake you up?"

Did it wake me up?

"It must have," I said, then changed the subject. "How're things in Helsinki?"

166

"Surely you know when the rain started since you've been spending all your time here, working."

His eyes were as impenetrable as always. The contempt was there, but he was also looking at me with curiosity and sincere interest.

"To tell you the truth," I said, "I think I fell asleep as soon as you left and slept until the evening. It was definitely raining by then."

"Sleeping during working hours?" His voice wasn't annoyed or shocked. Just the opposite. He looked genuinely amused. "Should I take it out of your pay?" he asked, then said, "I'm joking, Aleksi. I'm not interested in counting your hours. Far from it. I like you. I see a lot of myself in you. You know what you want, and you don't trouble yourself with irrelevancies. And most importantly, you're willing to take risks."

That last sentence was left to echo in my ears. It could be taken a thousand different ways.

"Speaking of risks," I said. "I know it's none of my business, but what was that private eye here about?"

Saarinen looked out at the sea.

"Something was stolen from me, and I want it back."

The book of poems. It had to be the book of poems. With my mother's name in it. Which I'd kept.

"What kind of theft do you mean?" I asked. "Did someone break into the house?"

"A break-in would be a police matter, wouldn't it?"

Saarinen took a couple of steps towards me and leaned on the railing with both hands, but his right hand was too tender. He visibly flinched in pain. His hand withdrew, trembling. I could only see part of the left side of his face, the edge of his mouth, the line of his chin. They seemed to convulse in pain. The hand slowly lowered to his side, as if he were being careful not to hurt it again.

I didn't say anything. An almost transparent screen of cloud lingered in front of the sun. I hoped he would keep talking. A moment later he started again.

"It's a personal possession, something that is only valuable to me. It would be hard to explain to someone if it was just a job to him. I mean it might be difficult to motivate him to get it back for me."

"I understand."

"Do you?" Saarinen said, not looking at me.

"Yes," I said. "You've hired someone to find it because he'll be motivated by money. You can pay him directly for returning it to you."

"That's not exactly what I meant," Saarinen said, turning towards me. It was a slow turn; he was clearly being careful of his hand. Whatever had happened to it, the wound must have been serious, or at least painful. When he'd made his half-turn, he leaned his back against the railing. The sea was behind him, his large head and powerful gaze set against a horizon filled with sky.

"I'm talking about the thing itself. It's a sort of memento. Do you have any of those? Objects that just look like objects, cheap, worthless, out of fashion, not fit for any decor, but they have a value to you because they remind you of some time or some person and they have a sort of feeling around them, a sort of energy field that makes them more than what they are — a broken toy truck, an old coin purse, or a chair that you can't sit in any more?"

"Doesn't everybody?"

"I'm asking you."

A seagull screeched somewhere nearby, but unseen. I thought of the bows, one tied by my mother, the other by some other person. The vase I'd put the two ribbons in, and of course the book that had called to me from the library shelf.

"Yes, I do."

"Then you know what I'm talking about."

The seagull cawed again.

"Are those things still in the car?" Saarinen asked, as if he'd already forgotten what we were just talking about.

"Still there," I said with a nod.

"Good. And are the keys in the box by the door?"

"Yes."

"So everything's ready."

I didn't know what he meant. He was still facing me directly. The arc of blue sky and the multilayered brightness of the water behind him made it impossible to see his eyes. He moved his right hand in front of him slowly, lifted it to chest height, as if to support it. Then he lowered it and lifted his head and must have been looking at me.

"Do you ever have the feeling that some thing or some idea has imprisoned you? As if in the middle of this beautiful place on this bright day there's a dark cloud over you and a dark, bottomless vacuum beneath you? That no matter how deeply you breathe in the fresh air, or look at the beautiful landscape, you'll never feel a part of that beauty, a part of the world?"

"I guess everybody has . . ."

"I'm asking you."

I knew the feeling he was talking about, but saying so felt like a defeat somehow, repugnant.

"Yes, I have."

"I knew you would understand," he said and turned his head just enough that he must have been looking not at me but at something across the yard, the maple tree or the woods. "I've actually always felt that way. Except in certain short moments. It's like drowning on dry land. Or like being shut up in such a small space that the key in your hand is no use because you can't move to use it. Like a dream where you're running from something but your feet won't obey you and you try to yell but nothing comes out because your mouth won't open and your tongue doesn't work and you can't make a sound."

Saarinen moved his bandaged hand in a small, sideways motion, as if testing to see if he still had the pain, if it was still waiting there. Clearly it still hurt as much as it had a moment before.

"Which brings up the only real question: are you ready to do whatever it takes to get free? Ready to act — even though you might endanger everything, might lose everything — in order to be able even for just a moment, just a few breaths, to breathe freely, to look around you and see what's in front of you as if for the first time?"

I didn't speak. Saarinen's large head nodded slowly.

"Sure you are. I know you are just by looking at you. These aren't the sort of things that are written on a resumé, summed up in a few words for people who won't understand it anyway. You either recognise it or you don't. I fought for a long time against my natural desires. I tried to make myself over into something I'm not, something that I thought I should be, should become. It didn't work. It just made the prison smaller, more stifling. Struggling just tightened the chains, pulled the net closer around me. Am I talking too much?"

He moved away from the sea side of the terrace, took a few steps towards me, and stood a couple of metres away. The smell of the air, the damp fragrance of the forest, and some aroma of burnt wood that clung to the sauna combined with his aftershave, a smell that drew my thoughts away from the seashore and into gleaming steel elevators and glass-walled conference rooms and made the situation feel even more contradictory.

"Not at all," I said, honestly.

Saarinen looked at me for a moment in silence, wiped something from his cheek with his uninjured hand, maybe some nonexistent bit of dirt or rain drop that had dried yesterday. There was in his eyes in addition to the curiosity, something soft and open, which in a different situation I would have interpreted as a need for help.

"Everyone wants to be free, Aleksi. Everyone wants to get out of their prison. It won't happen until we understand where the prison is. It's in the same place for everyone. Between your ears. We blame our pasts,

171

things that were done to us, or some thing or some person that has prevented us from doing what we really want to do. We'd rather be prisoners than take responsibility for freeing ourselves."

This two-metre-tall man, speaking in a level voice, expressionless, sounded like Paulo Coelho's psychopath brother, but he was apparently in earnest, and I needed every crumb of knowledge I could get, every shred of a clue that would lead me forward. I was trying to think of a natural way to answer or add something to these meditations, when Saarinen became interested in something else and took a few steps forward and to the right. With amazing nimbleness he picked up the knife out of Amanda's fish bucket and straightened up again. Then he turned away, walked over the squeaking floorboards back to the railing, stopped, and stood standing with his back to me.

"And yet we're willing to do so little," he said, putting the knife down on the top of the railing. The movement was a careful one. He stepped away, leaving about half a metre between himself and the knife. The arrangement seemed as carefully constructed as a pose for a painting: an unidentified, broad-shouldered man standing with his back to the viewer, a railing, a knife, and in the background the wide, open sea. It was an effort to hear his voice. He was facing the water.

"It's more than twenty years since I first understood what I had to do to free myself. Afterwards I measured my life according to that: I made plans, waited, and finally acted, and for moments was able to feel the warmth of the sun on my face, my thoughts flying and grateful, like I meant them to be. Free for a moment, no longer locked in a prison, drowning in a cramped, airless, dark little barrel."

I was silent.

"You see this knife, Aleksi?"

I said I did. The blade shone in the sun and the yellow handle was like a slice of fresh lemon.

"What would you like to do with it? If you could do whatever you wanted, what would you do? Would you use it to free yourself? Would you be ready to do that?"

I looked at the knife, its graceful shape, its sharp point. The longer, the more closely I looked at it, the more inviting it seemed. Something in its presence, the thing it was made for — stabbing, cutting, slicing, dividing, opening — was compelling my hand towards it, and somewhere in my mind was an urge, a growing image, or series of images, fragments of myself lunging at Saarinen, picking up the knife in my hand, gripping the handle so hard my knuckles were white, my fingers hurt, like a series of moving photographs, hacking at him swiftly, not caring where I struck, just to get out of the situation, to speed up the thing that was going to happen anyway.

I made myself remain calm. For what I was here for. Saarinen turned slowly. The sun bathed his large face, turned it golden, soft and round.

"Aleksi, what do you want to be?"

Those were my mother's words.

AUGUST 1993

My mother's lipstick is as red as movie blood. She's sitting on a chair by the door wearing her best clothes. Her high-heeled shoes shine like black pearls. They don't stay still for more than a second or two. Her fingernails are the same red as her lips. She brushes her clean white sleeve as if she wished there were something on it — a hair, a tiny speck of dust — and looks at the clock.

We're both waiting: my mother's waiting for someone she's excited to see, and I'm waiting for a lift to a football match. My sports bag is in the doorway, like a dog waiting to go for its walk.

My mother radiates a nervousness she's trying to conceal. I'm not used to seeing her like this. It makes me nervous, too, and reinforces the peculiar feeling that's been growing all day.

It's pouring with rain outside, coming down in sheets and lashing against the windows when the wind gusts. I've spent the whole day indoors because of it. So has my mother, who is on her last week of holiday. Somehow today feels like the end of the holiday, although the week's only half over and school won't start for another week and a half. Not just the end of the break, though. I feel as if something else were ending, too. I don't know what.

She gets up from the chair and stands in front of the mirror again. I see her eyes in it. They shine through her dark make-up like stars. Her eyes find mine. She doesn't turn around, just looks at me in the mirror. She tries to smile.

Who are you playing against?

It's just the sort of behaviour that makes me nervous. She's been like this all day. Asked me the same question three times. I'm sure she doesn't hear me when I say again: Gnistan.

Her next question shows that she did hear me after all.

In Oulunkylä?

Yep.

Even though it's raining?

Yep.

I know what the coach and the fathers who show up will say. *Just a few sprinkles. Get on the field. We're playing.* That's fine with me. At the moment a rainy, muddy football pitch sounds more appealing than anywhere else, near or far. I'm stuck indoors. I need to get out under the sky. At the same time I realise that not all my restlessness is because of the rainy day. I look at my mother and my nervousness immediately increases.

Where are you going?

Her gaze bounces off the mirror like a puck from the wall of an ice hockey rink.

I'm going out.

Who with?

An acquaintance. I'll be home about the same time you are. We can eat then.

Why won't you tell me your acquaintance's name?

She stops combing her hair, lowers her hand to her side, turns around and looks at me. She isn't smiling. She looks determined.

I will tell you. This evening, for sure. I think I might have another thing to tell you then, too.

I'm thirteen years old and I understand something about human relationships. I know, for instance, that everything is not always what it seems, not by a long shot, and that sometimes things can get complicated and people can reveal things that are usually kept hidden.

What sort of thing?

Her face turns more serious.

You know what's most important to me. You. And our home. You'll remember that, won't you?

I nod.

I've wanted to protect you, and this home.

She comes and stands in front of me and puts her hand on my shoulder, next to my neck. The perfume she's rubbed on her wrist smells like oranges and the lilacs in the yard. She looks so deep into my eyes that everything else disappears.

And I would never bring anyone here if I didn't feel they were important. That's why I haven't told you this person's name. Only important people can have a

176

name. But even if they do end up having a name or visiting here, none of them will ever come before you.

Then she does something she hasn't done in a while. She presses her hands over my ears and kisses me on the top of the head. I think that my head will have red lipstick marks that someone taller than me will see. The rain feels even more inviting now. She straightens up, looks at her watch again, and goes to the mirror to fix her lipstick and take her thin, black coat off the hook. She ties a red scarf around her neck and picks up her umbrella. She still hasn't answered my question. I still feel a tremendous uneasiness inside.

Don't go, I say, surprising even myself. Words that I didn't expect, that sum up all the nervous tension of the day. They're the right words, I realise.

She turns around. She smiles. A warm smile.

We'll see each other in a few hours. Have a good game.

Wait, I say, quickly pulling my shoes on and heaving my bag over my shoulder.

What's the rush?

I don't say anything. I don't know the answer, don't know what the rush is, or if there is one. I just need to go out of the door when she does. We walk down the four flights of stairs. We have a rule, or actually not a rule but a game — we only use the elevator if we have something heavy to carry and we're going up. We follow the rule that's not a rule this time, too.

The asphalt courtyard is like a lake. We stand in the foyer.

Aleksi, is everything all right?

Suddenly I know what I should say, but just then Vesa's father's Saab 900 honks its horn and I have to run.

I get soaked on the way to the car and forget for ever what it was that I was going to say to my mother. But not quite for ever.

Just for twenty years.

SEPTEMBER 2013

Not everything is what it seems to be.

The words that were left unsaid. The words that could hardly have meant anything to anyone, that could hardly have prevented what happened later, what had to happen.

I could smell autumn in the air. The sea shimmered and rippled like a rug woven from silver. Henrik Saarinen was waiting for my answer.

"I prefer to be what I am," I said. "A maintenance man. I don't want to be anything else. I don't want to become anything else."

Saarinen tilted his head. He was a man in love with his own ideas, his own voice and thoughts, having someone nearby to hear them and see them. He loved playing this game. One way or another he was going to beat me. The game would go on for as long as I refused to give in.

"You refuse to evolve," he said. "Even though you don't know what it is that I'm offering."

"Even if I did know, I would still be what I am."

Saarinen smiled. A smile like rotten fruit.

"Shall we make a bet?"

"I don't think I can afford —"

"Not for money," he said.

"For what then?"

The seagull, which I'd thought gone, screeched again. Who was it screeching at? It was alone in the sky.

"Today's Tuesday. On Friday evening I'll take you somewhere. If what you see then, what you experience, doesn't change your opinion, then I lose. If after that evening you still want to be a caretaker and nothing more, I'll tell you what you want to know."

The terrace we were standing on started to rock underneath me. It felt as if it would come off its supports and move across the water, where it would tip and try to knock us off. I was sure that the sky would change colour, go dark, turn completely black and drown us both in darkness. The vertigo lasted for half a second and I was standing firm again on the broad wood floor, looking at Henrik Saarinen. He had a curious, expectant look on his face.

"How do you know there's anything I want to know?" I asked.

"There is."

"Then why not tell me now?"

"That wouldn't suit either one of us. As I said before, I see something in you that's more than just a maintenance man. I see something you can't see yourself. Do you believe in coincidences?"

Amanda's question.

"No," I said.

"It just so happens that I don't either. Friday night at nine. Don't make any other plans."

180

The curiosity and interest had disappeared from his face, replaced by insistence.

"All right," I said. "Friday night. Do I need to —"

"You don't need to worry about anything except being here. It's an evening I've been planning for ten years."

Having said this, he took his phone out of his pocket and looked at it. I hadn't heard it ring, or even vibrate, but he saw something there that made him raise his eyebrows.

"Friday, then," he said, walking past me and leaving me on the terrace.

His aftershave lingered in the air for a moment with its sweet-sour smell. I heard his steps recede the same way they'd come. The sky was blue except for random shreds of cotton fluff and scattered curls of cloud. The seagull screamed again. It flew directly above me and glided between shore and water. The pale grey bird couldn't decide whether to trust its wings and head out to sea or stay safely close to the land.

I did the rest of my day's work: cleaned the rain gutters, cut some more firewood, oiled the dry, squeaking hinges and took down a painting scaffold left on the west end of the toolshed that had been standing there for several winters and wasn't good for anything now but being broken up and burned.

From the outside I'm sure I looked like someone diligently absorbed in his work. But the physical work was secondary.

I was waiting.

SEPTEMBER 2013

I was waiting, even though my whole being felt as if it was coming apart at the seams. How could years of uncertainty be made certain? Did I need an earth-shattering, sudden revelation of absolute truth, or was the picture emerging piece by piece enough?

I couldn't reach Ketomaa by phone any more. Amanda wasn't answering my calls.

It had been a long night full of fragmented, confusing dreams. I woke up feeling hungover, although I hadn't drunk a drop.

I turned over Saarinen's words and manner from the day before in my mind. I kept hearing his voice, seeing his bandaged hand. Everything seemed to add up to one thing: his talk about waiting for ten years, telling me to leave the tools in the back of the SUV, his attitude towards me — fatherly, as if he was talking to a pupil, wanting to show me something that he thought would change the direction of my life — and the fact that he clearly knew more about me than I wanted him to know.

I washed up the dishes, got dressed, and was just about to go out when I heard someone coming up the stairs. The steps sounded familiar, but I was still surprised. I hadn't heard a car arrive. I waited for a knock, then opened the door.

Markus Harmala didn't look as if he had come about a work matter. He wasn't in uniform, in any case. His demeanour was also not commensurate with official business. Maybe it was his 1990s playboy outfit — a white hoodie, light blue "distressed" jeans, and bright white running shoes — or maybe it was his body language, trying to look self-confident but coming over as arrogant, striving for a position where he could look down on me, which, since we were the same height, came across like a teenage challenge. Or maybe it was the combination of all of these things.

I didn't want a fight. I'd gone too far on the street that night. Acted without thinking. I couldn't afford that.

"We left some unfinished business in Eira, handyman," Harmala said.

I waved him inside. He walked to the middle of the room and looked around.

"I don't think I've ever been in here," he said. "Cute place. It suits you."

"I'm happy with it."

He took his time turning around.

"Are you," he said, not sounding as if he was asking a question. His eyes held mine, staring me down. "You like living here? Working as a caretaker?"

"Yes."

"And you just happened to be driving around the other night? Is that right?"

He shoved his hands in his pockets and struck a more relaxed pose.

"Yes," I said.

When we didn't speak I could hear the wind in the trees outside, the hum of the refrigerator, my own breathing. Harmala pulled out a chair and sat down at the table. He seemed to be waiting for me to do the same. I did. The brightening day was reflected in the woodgrain of the table, warm and flowing like waves on water.

"I've been here since 1993," Harmala said. "When I was eighteen I was invited for an interview. Henrik interviewed me himself and hired me. Personally. I know these people, and this place."

The light came into the room from the window beside us, illuminating only one side of his face. In this new light, he looked different, which was strange, since I'd spent so much time in his company when I was following Saarinen years ago. I'd never looked at him from this angle before, never noticed his slightly yellow complexion, his features, that hairline.

"I've seen all kinds of things over the years," he said. "And all kinds of people. Working here, and other places. The rich attract all sorts."

Another heavy silence. Harmala put his elbows on the table.

"Especially rich, young, beautiful women."

I looked him in the eye. I knew this was why he'd come.

"I'm not here because of Amanda, if that's what you mean."

184

He looked as if he were thinking about what I'd said.

"Still just a handyman?"

"Still just a handyman."

He leaned back in his chair. He seemed always to be searching for a better observation point, something to help him take control of the situation, control of the other person. He ended up looking at me with his head tilted towards the window.

"That's all?"

"I could ask you whether you're just here as a driver."

He scratched his smooth cheek.

"I'm going to be straight with you," he said, ignoring my question. "You might be able to bullshit Henrik, and even Amanda, but not me. You're no more a caretaker than I'm a member of the yacht club."

I looked at him. I was thinking about what he'd said. That he'd started working here the same year that my mother disappeared. He'd been eighteen years old. A young man, but a legal adult.

"You can check up on me," I said. "I'm a carpenter, have been for ten years. I was hired to work here after several interviews. Elias Ahlberg must have told you that."

"I'm not interested in hearing about your past. I'm interested in you leaving here and . . . and leaving Amanda alone. Disappearing from her life, from all our lives."

"Let's leave Amanda out of this —"

"Let's leave Amanda out of this," he said mockingly. "The fuck we will. You're talking like a man in love. Either you leave or . . ."

He left the sentence unfinished, looked at me for a second, and stood up. He walked to the door, seemed about to say something, but didn't. He slammed the door as he left.

I spent the morning hauling gravel in a wheelbarrow, tipping it out load by load next to the dock, close to the water's edge, to widen and shore up the finger of land. The air was cool, the day bright. I worked in my T-shirt. I enjoyed using my muscles, sweating, feeling the sea wind on my skin, breathing deep lungfuls of air. I warmed up some of Enni's leftover lasagne in the microwave, ate it, drank two cups of coffee, and walked back down to the shore, where the sky was already a little darker blue than it had been an hour or two earlier.

If I had to choose — or if anyone had ever asked me — I would have said that autumn is my favourite time of year. When the light is rich, nature is at its most delicate and fresh, the air is warm, but purified by nights of rain, the leaves madly glowing, the forest aromatic with the combination of wet and dry, and the blue canopy of cloudless sky is deep and intoxicating. In the city, too, life is lived fullest in September. The unhurried days of summer are over but the cold of winter hasn't yet arrived to sweep them away. The sweltering heat is gone but the biting cold hasn't yet come to subdue your spirit. I've always thought September was the most hopeful month, full of promise and unfolding possibility.

When evening came and I'd finished my day's work, I remembered what Enni had said when I went for some food the day before. When everyone who needed her services had gone she would be leaving Kalmela for a couple of days and I would be left alone there. She'd asked if I had any questions about the estate, and I almost said something clever, but I didn't want to be cheeky any more. I thanked her for the food and said with all honesty that I didn't have any questions and that everything was clear to me. She looked at me, waiting for me to make a mistake, to blurt out something I thought was funny so she could sniff and disapprove. But I didn't. Maybe I made an impression on her. There was a new interest, a sharper look in her eyes.

"How are things otherwise?" she asked.

It was the first time I'd heard anything other than defensiveness and disappointment in her voice. I said things were great. She looked at me a moment longer and I could see the friendliness disappear again. As if she'd noticed something in me that she had disregarded before.

"I'm glad to hear it," she said, but she didn't sound glad at all. I could see that she wanted to ask me something else, something completely different, but the moment had passed and we went our separate ways.

I sat by the window and watched the sunset, the lights coming on in front of the main house. The yellow glow was like a seam of gold. In the dark the place looked bigger than it really was. Against the fading violet horizon it reminded me of a little castle that history had cast aside, like everything else.

The sun went down. A fat, glowing full moon settled over the forest.

I didn't see or hear Enni's car leave, but at some point it had disappeared from its place in the parking area in front of the house. I waited another half hour, then left my apartment and went down the stairs to the edge of the yard. I stopped and looked around. I didn't see any people or cars. Enni had been right. I was alone. At last.

I opened the door of the main house with my key, ready to feed the code into the alarm system, and I was surprised. Enni must have forgotten to turn it on.

I walked through the foyer with its stairs leading to the first floor on one side and the broad doorway on the right that led into the room they called the hall. I listened. I'd studied the sounds of the house all the time I'd spent there. Every time I had some reason to be there I'd watched and listened, trying to learn all its sounds, smells, moods, dimensions. I was sure that the house could tell me something about what had happened twenty years before, but it was silent now.

I was about to turn on the light, but thought better of it. I had brought a powerful torch with me, there was a full moon outside, and I had done my homework. I wouldn't stumble on a threshold or trip over the furniture — I had the blueprint of the place clearly in my mind. And if someone pulled into the driveway and saw the lights on, I would have to explain myself.

Again. No thanks. I intended to explore places I had no permission to be in.

So I let my eyes adjust to the gloom. I'd seen the place in daylight, now I wanted to know what it could tell me in the dark. I climbed the stairs to the first floor, avoiding the centre of the steps, which I knew would creak. My moonlit walk was careful and quiet. I could see the pictures on the walls, the shapes of chairs and cabinets, could feel the rugs and wood floors under my feet. Why was I moving silently if I knew I was alone in the house? The fact that the alarm was off was still bothering me. I took a deep breath and assured myself there was no one else there.

The first floor was like a museum in the moonlight. The antique and faux antique furniture looked as if it was on display. I chose a route close to the wall again, because the centre of the floor wheezed and creaked in complaint as if I was stepping on a living thing. The first room I passed was a guest room. I would come back to it later.

At the door to Saarinen's bedroom I stopped.

The room had been turned upside down. The closets and dressers were open, their contents dumped in piles in front of them, then kicked and hurled across the room. The bed was stripped of its bedding and the mattresses thrown against the wall. The bare antique bed frame looked like the foundation of a small house. Not a single object was left on the tables, they had all been thrown on the floor, the tables pulled away from the walls, their backs turned to the front. Some of the drawers were pulled from their cabinets entirely. The bookshelves were empty, the books lying on the floor in front of them. The shelves themselves were pulled away from the wall, too. The pictures left on the walls hung at crazy angles so extreme that they looked as if they were purposely placed that way. The entire contents of the bedside table had been emptied onto the floor, down to the last bottle of sleeping pills. The pills gleamed in the moonlight like tiny stones.

It must have been about an hour since Enni left. I'd come into the house about ten minutes ago. This had happened sometime in between.

When I was completely sure that I could still move with the same soft soundlessness as before, I slowly turned around. I let my gaze sweep over the landing. I didn't see anyone hiding, no bulge under the curtains, no one crouching behind the sofa or sitting calmly in an easy chair. I didn't see or hear anyone. I didn't feel the presence of anyone.

The rest of the house was still in good order, perfectly clean, only Henrik Saarinen's room looked as if it had been struck by a tornado.

I turned to look at the ransacked room again. I listened again, as hard as I could. Since I could no more tell Saarinen about the mess than I could the police, I might as well leave. But not yet.

The room told me at least two things. Henrik Saarinen had something that somebody wanted, and that somebody must not have found what they were looking for. If they had, they would have stopped tearing the place apart. The room was turned upside down from one end to the other, so the search must have been unsuccessful.

I closed the blinds on the windows. I turned on my torch and began with the contents of the bedside table. I'd noticed the sleeping pills, but there were other things from the drawer on the floor. Most of them were what you would expect to find in a bedside table — old art reprint postcards with nothing written on them, two gold wristwatches, an assortment of notebooks and calendars, handkerchiefs, eyedrops, two kinds of lotion.

Ballpoint pens with restaurant logos. One of them seemed familiar. The South Pier Restaurant. A waterfront establishment. I put the pen in my coat pocket.

I found a pillowcase torn from its pillow on the floor and used it to cover my hands while I leafed through the calendars and notebooks. They were all empty. Every single page. I threw down the pillowcase. I swept the beam of the torch over the bed, looked behind the shelves and tables that had been pulled from the walls and at the bookshelves' contents scattered on the floor. Nothing caught my attention like the pen had.

It was time to leave.

I turned off the torch, adjusted to the dark again for a moment, and opened the blinds. The light of the moon flooded the room. It looked the same as it had when I came in. My steps were still soft and soundless as I went out to the landing and walked close to the wall past the guest room. One glance inside was enough. Everything was in its place, nothing touched. Light poured through the large windows onto the landing; the space was almost as bright as day. Everything was immaculately clean. And immaculately silent. I placed my steps carefully on the rug.

Then I felt something on my skin. A draught. There must be a door or a window open somewhere. I made a quick, silent circuit of the first floor. No one, no open doors or windows. I listened again, but all I could hear was myself and the sounds of the house, all of them in their expected places, every creak and click that an old house makes.

I went back to the top of the stairs, turned the torch in my hand to get a better grip for what might be waiting downstairs — a broken window, an open door, an intruder.

I took a breath, lifted my right foot, ready to lower it onto the first step, when the step disappeared. I felt two side blows to my back, and instead of my foot landing on a broad step, I went sideways into emptiness, groping the air, and my torch fell out of my hand.

SEPTEMBER 2013

"Do you need a doctor?"

The world didn't want to stay still. When I turned my head to the right everything careened in the opposite direction, but if I held my head straight it lurched top over bottom. The left side of my face was numb. Touching it with my fingertips I could feel that the rough carpet I was lying on had left deep grooves in my skin. The shy light of a new morning crept through the windows as if it were feeling for an angle of approach.

I struggled into a sitting position. I remembered the two blows to my back.

"Are you all right?"

Another question I couldn't answer. I managed to make the carousel slow down. Even at high speed, though, I would have recognised Mansikka-aho's red eyes.

"How did you get here?" I asked. My mouth was dry as a sunburned leaf. It tasted like one, too.

"Through the door," he said.

"What door?"

"The front door. It was open. I came inside. I saw you."

I scrambled to my feet, holding on to the bannister.

"Have you been here all night?" Mansikka-aho asked. "Did you sleep here?"

I didn't answer. His presence couldn't mean anything good. And I didn't have any clever Marloweisms to toss off in any case.

"Are you alone in the house?"

He was full of questions. I couldn't look him in the eye for more than a second or two before the carousel started to spin again and I had to concentrate on balancing and breathing. I needed a glass of water. I started down the stairs, arrived at the bottom, and decided to go to the kitchen. I glanced behind me as I crossed the wide obstacle of the hall. Mansikka-aho followed with his hands in the pockets of his leather jacket. Had he really just arrived? It was hard to read anything from his face or demeanour. It was as if he were permanently hidden beneath his stubble and bloodshot eyes.

I made it to the kitchen, turned on the tap, and searched for the largest possible glass from the cupboard. My thirst had grown from severe to prodigious. I drank and Mansikka-aho watched me. If the previous few days hadn't been so full of unexpected events I would have thought the situation peculiar, perhaps even employed the overused term surreal, but now it was just one more event in my life — a police detective watching me drink water from a millionaire's glass. The clock on the wall showed half past seven.

"You're up early," I said.

Mansikka-aho stood squarely facing me, his hands still in his pockets and his eyes fixed on mine. He

194

looked as if he wouldn't give an inch under any circumstances.

"And you work here. You didn't tell me that when we met. What's happened?"

"Nothing," I said.

"Right. You always sleep on the upstairs landing. The door was open and there was no one here. What happened?"

Hadn't he seen the upstairs?

"Nothing. I felt weak this morning. I must have fainted."

"When?"

"Just now," I said. "I left the door open when I came in."

I couldn't tell from his face whether he believed me. He was thinking about it.

"What about Ketomaa? Is he here?"

"No."

"But he knows you're working here?"

"Yes. Is it all right to ask a cop what he's doing somewhere?"

"Of course."

"What are you doing here?"

"I'm looking for Ketomaa. Like I said."

"Don't you people usually come in pairs? You're out alone."

"Why wouldn't I be? This doesn't seem to be a dangerous place."

Walking to the kitchen I'd been thinking that my time was up, that now Saarinen was going to find out who I was and why I was here. But Mansikka-aho wasn't behaving like a snitch. Maybe it was true that he was here looking for Ketomaa.

"What makes you think Ketomaa might be here?"

"What do you think? Henrik Saarinen, of course. Does Saarinen know who you are?"

"No."

"Are you sure?"

He looked at me with his red eyes. Somebody must have already suggested eyedrops, so I wasn't going to start. Was I sure? Of course not, but this was no time for speculation.

"Yes," I said. "Are you going to tell him?"

Mansikka-aho didn't answer.

"When did you last see Ketomaa here?" he asked.

I told him briefly and as honestly as I could about our recent meeting in front of the house. When I'd finished he said, "Be careful about that dizziness. If it catches you in the wrong place you could seriously injure yourself."

I followed him outside, where the autumn morning was waiting, so crisp, so dazzlingly bright and bracingly clear that it made you want to walk into it like walking into someone's arms. The trees stood peaceful in the still air, steady, as if they believed that they could keep their beautiful red and yellow leaves for ever.

Mansikka-aho looked around as we approached his car. He was clearly able to completely ignore the beautiful day. He looked gloomy. Before he got in the car he said that if I saw Ketomaa I should let him know as soon as possible.

196

I promised I would. He started the car and pulled out of the yard.

I watched him drive away and wondered how I had managed to appear so calm, inside the house when he'd found me and peppered me with questions, and above all now, in front of the house, bathed in the pure light of the rising sun as his white Ford receded into the distance.

I found the pen I'd taken from Saarinen's room in my pocket. Whoever it was who gave me a push, at least he hadn't gone through my pockets. I turned on my phone. Seven text messages received.

Something happened. Call me.
I know that Harmala came to see you.
My father was here.
He's done something sick.
Where the fuck are you?
Good night you fucking piece of shit.
I get it. You're a prick, just like all the others.

To make love to a woman who had a black eye and a fat lip wasn't what I had planned, but that's what happened.

After I read the texts I drove to Helsinki, jammed the car into a restricted zone and walked with firm steps to Amanda's apartment. This time she'd left the door open. I found her in the bedroom and immediately took my clothes off.

Our lovemaking was sticky and grasping. As if we were afraid that the other person would escape. I didn't

197

want to look at Amanda's purplish, swollen eye or her split lower lip. I kissed her neck and her breasts and kept my eyes closed.

"He came late yesterday evening," she said when I'd finally wrenched myself away from her. "Around eleven or so. I wondered why he was here. He never comes here. Especially not late at night. He said we absolutely had to talk. I said OK. And at first we just talked. Like a father and daughter. How have you been, what are you going to do with your life. He asked me that, I mean. He always asks me that. I don't want to know what he has in mind. Then he started telling me what I ought to be doing. Again. And I can't stand that, I hate it. No one tells me what to do."

She was quiet for a moment. I turned my head. The swollen eye made it hard to look at her. In some strange way she seemed proud of her injuries, even seemed to be enjoying the situation. Or maybe I was misinterpreting everything, maybe I was still more off balance than I realised.

"I told him he could take his advice and shove it up his ass. Then I said it was no wonder my mother left him, left the country entirely so she wouldn't have to look at him and listen to him, he's such a pig. He got angry. He started accusing me of all sorts of things. Explaining how he had done all he could for me. I said is that why you fucked every woman in town and spread your seed everywhere, for the good of the family? I didn't know it was such a sore spot, but I guess it was, because then he hit me."

My gaze wandered over the walls. Over their broad, white surfaces, straight and simple in a way that was starting to feel more enviable the longer I looked at them. The yellow light from the bedside table gave the high-ceilinged room a softness that made you want to touch it.

"He hit me several times," I heard Amanda saying. "Yelling, barking at me."

Her chest rose and fell. The muscles of her thin frame were tense, in spite of the fact that she was lying on her back.

"This is the last straw. Do you understand, Aleksi?"

The blinds hid whatever sky I might have seen. The frames of the windows looked sad and useless, without day or night.

"Aleksi? Are you listening to me?"

"Of course I am," I said, not turning my head.

"What did I say?"

"The last straw," I said. It sounded like my own voice on a recording, irritatingly familiar and startlingly strange.

Amanda rolled onto her side. I knew she was looking at me.

"This isn't the first time. I know that's why my mother left him. She was afraid. Of course she was, living with a monster."

I didn't look at Amanda. I asked, "What do you remember about 1993?"

"What did you say?"

"What do you remember about it? 1993? Your mother left nineteen years ago, in '94. What do you remember about the time before that?"

"You really are crazy, aren't you? Look at me. Look at my eye and my lip."

I turned my head. Amanda Saarinen, the millionaire heiress, with a shiner and a swollen lip like a street scrapper. Henrik Saarinen, my mother, 1993. It was all coming together. I was so close I felt dizzy. Tomorrow Henrik would be mine.

"Did your mother ever say what she was afraid of? What particularly she feared?"

"I just told you. She was afraid of my father. I was afraid of my father. I still am."

"This has to do with your eye," I said, putting a hand on her cheek. Up close I could see something in her left nostril. A tiny white spot. "And your lip. Tell me what you remember."

"My father's a pig. I've had enough."

"I believe you. But what about 1993?"

She turned her back to me.

"They had their own lives. I didn't understand anything back then, but I do now. I know they had their own lovers, for instance. Then something happened that finally made the old witch say good riddance. She was afraid, even though she was nearly as frightening herself. To a little girl, I mean. But that was then. I'm not a frightened little girl any more."

"No, you're not," I said. "What do you think happened that made your mother finally leave?"

Amanda took a deep breath in, then out. I watched her chest rise and fall.

"Aleksi, remember when I asked you if you believed in coincidences?"

200

"Yes."

"You came into my life for a reason. I believe that my father at one time did something really shocking. Something really horrible. He can't . . . he has to stop . . ."

She stopped speaking and pulled the covers over herself. The room was cool. I hadn't noticed before. The white walls looked pure and pleasing, but as soon as you noticed the temperature they seemed hard and impenetrable. Amanda's talk excited me, tempted me to ask more questions. I tried to keep myself in check.

"Horrible how?" I asked, sounding as unconcerned as I could.

She looked as if she expected the question.

"I'm certain he hurt someone, maybe even killed someone."

The room went quiet. The normal sounds of an apartment house — a flushing toilet, a couple arguing, a child's footsteps across the floor above, the heavy beats from a bachelor's boom box — were missing. Nothing was moving or living. Is this how it would all come together, this easily?

"When?" I asked. "In 1993?"

"Yeah."

"You don't sound sure."

"But I am sure. I mean, I'm sure about 2003."

Her face was turned away from me towards the window. That was good. I braced myself on an elbow.

"You may not remember it," she said, "but it was in all the newspapers. A woman named Tanja Metsäpuro. My father dated her. Then she was killed. It was never talked about in our house. And I remember once when we were at Kalmela and we were sitting in the hall and there was some tabloid on the table with a big picture of her. When my father saw me looking at it he turned the paper over with the photo facing down and he looked at me in this scary way and we didn't say a word about it."

Amanda still had her back to me. I couldn't see her face.

"Did you ever ask about it?"

"Of course not. Because he could do the same thing to me." She turned and looked at me. "I've never told this to anyone."

"Why are you telling me now?"

She pressed up against my side and whispered, her lips nearly touching my ear.

"Because you can fix it."

The white walls receded. Her bare skin felt hot.

"How?"

"I'll ask you straight," she said, so quietly that it was like a part of her breathing. "Will you kill him?"

SEPTEMBER 1993

My mother calls them our home nights, although we're at home a lot of nights, almost every night in fact. Home nights include a movie, which we choose together or draw straws to decide who will choose. She gets the long straw this time.

It's Friday night; she's taken a sauna. She has curlers in her hair and is wearing her bathrobe. I've already eaten, a gut bomb I made myself with four frankfurters seasoned with mustard and pickle relish and a dash of ketchup. I can still taste it in my mouth hours later.

My mother puts her slice of toast on her plate and tops it with Turunmaa cheese, pours herself a glass of wine, and sets the plate and glass on the table. She sits in the armchair and I start the video.

She says this is her favourite movie.

I fear the worst.

She likes old movies and a lot of them are the kind of thing I find boring: black and white with crackly sound or colour with endless dialogue, tense close-ups of tense conversations.

This one is different from anything I've ever seen.

It's like watching a bad dream that you want to see all the way to the end.

The movie starts with a chase scene. The police are chasing a thief across the rooftops of tall buildings. One of the policemen slips and hangs from the rain gutter, his life on the line. A cop in a suit tries to help and falls to his death. The man who was hanging there survives, but he quits the police department. An old schoolmate gets in touch with him. He gets a job following the old schoolmate's wife. The schoolmate, who is now a rich businessman, asks if the dead can take control of the living.

I glance at my mother. Her glass of wine stops on its way to her lips.

The man follows the woman around San Francisco. For an excruciatingly long time.

At the part where the woman suddenly jumps into the ocean, my mother's face doesn't register a thing.

She watches me for a few seconds, smiles, lifts her eyebrows, and we continue watching.

He goes after her, saves her from drowning, they get to know each other, and they kiss. But the woman isn't OK. He tries to help her, takes her to different places — to a forest where giant trees grow, to a Spanish monastery, to a riding stable. They kiss all the time, over and over. The woman pulls herself away, climbs up a bell tower, throws herself off it, and dies. The man runs away.

I check the clock on the video player to see how long the movie's been playing and the cover of the video to see how much more there is. Still an hour to go.

204

There's more, I hear my mother say. Her face is inscrutable. She said this was her favourite movie.

There is indeed more.

The bad dream deepens.

I can't stop watching.

The man is a patient in some kind of mental hospital and he won't answer when his old girlfriend talks to him. The old girlfriend loves him, but he doesn't love her. He gets out of the hospital and sees the dead woman everywhere. He meets a woman on the street and starts to dress her to look like the dead woman.

My mother's face tenses. She pulls her feet up into the chair and wraps her arms around her legs, curling up in a tight ball. There's still a drop of red wine in her glass.

The woman writes a letter confessing everything. She's a con artist. Her husband killed his previous wife. She tears up the letter. She doesn't tell the man the truth, doesn't tell him anything.

The movie keeps going.

Keeps going?

Even though the riddle is solved!

Finally the woman looks like the dead woman. The man seems to have gone completely crazy, or maybe he's cured. It's hard to say.

My mother watches from under her eyelids, as if she's terribly afraid and is forcing herself to watch.

Why is she so tense if she's seen the movie before and knows what's going to happen? I ask.

This is a different kind of suspense.

What kind?

This movie is about more than just what happens.

Right.

Hush, she says.

The woman in the movie is in front of a mirror trying to put on a necklace. She asks the man to help her. He comes up behind her and looks in the mirror. He recognises the necklace. The man and the woman drive to the Spanish monastery, the same place where the woman jumped off the bell tower. The man drags her to the top of the tower. The woman confesses. Someone comes into the tower — a nun. The woman is so afraid that she dives out of the window, hits the roof tiles below, and dies.

The man is left standing on the top of the tower.

The end.

The end?

I look at my mother.

There may be tears in her eyes.

I feel cheated. I say so. I say that a story should have an ending, a proper ending.

Proper in what way? she asks.

I don't know.

I can't explain.

But not like that.

Why not?

Just not, I say quietly, testily. The criminal was never caught.

Sometimes that's the way it is. Sometimes the criminal doesn't get caught.

SEPTEMBER 2013

The edge of the sky glowed like a hot coal and the sun was just a thin sliver of boiling molten metal on the horizon as I came out onto Liisankatu and walked to my car. A darkening evening, long shadows, lots of places to hide. All these things should have warned me of the possibility of a surprise. Nevertheless, I was startled when I heard a familiar voice behind me.

"Where are you headed, Aleksi? Or more to the point, where are you coming from?"

Henrik Saarinen had parked his Land Cruiser behind a delivery van. That was why I hadn't noticed it. Now I could see its nose over his shoulder, glaringly familiar. Saarinen's face showed no trace of his usual smile or haughtiness. His expression was serious, a darkness in his eyes that I hadn't noticed before.

"I was bringing Amanda some things she forgot at Kalmela," I said.

Saarinen came closer and stopped a metre from me. "Is that all?"

He looked at me a little more openly, his head high. He still had a white bandage on his right hand. It showed bright against his black leather jacket, like a rolled-up white flag. The kind I didn't expect him to wave, ever. Not even if it was his last option.

"Well," he said. "Amanda got what she wanted. That's what's important."

He lifted his bandaged hand. Maybe it hurt and he needed to move it.

"We've had a little change in plans," he said.

"Yeah?"

"It can't wait. Leave your car here."

It didn't sound like a suggestion. The last rays of sun gilded his grey hair. His black jacket shone. Had my mother followed him as easily as this? Received an invitation and gone with him, without asking any questions?

That's how everything in life happens. Without our noticing, or thinking, while we're doing something else. Always in good faith.

Whenever I thought about my mother's fate — and when didn't I? — I'd always ignored the moment when she physically died, what that was like, how long it lasted. For some reason my thoughts had never reached that point. I could imagine the brutality, like everyone can imagine such things. I was capable of understanding the sorts of things that must have been done to her. But the moment of death escaped me, like a magnet repelling another, turning aside every time you try to push it closer.

Now that moment felt closer than ever before. The moment when a person leaves the world. One minute she exists, the next minute she doesn't.

"Can I ask you something?"

"When we get there."

"Where are we going?"

"When we get there."

Saarinen turned around, threw me the keys. I snatched them from the air. He went around the car as I clicked the doors open. I looked behind me one last time. The highest windows of the apartment house reflected the sky — purple, pink, and a stronger, more vivid blood and fire of red. The shadows had grown as long as they could grow and begun to mingle, forming lakes of black on the cobblestone street and asphalt pavement.

As I got in I glanced into the back of the car. The tools I'd bought at the hardware store were gone.

Henrik Saarinen fastened his seatbelt and hung onto the grab handle with his right hand as if preparing for a bumpy ride. He seemed remarkably calm considering that he'd beaten up his daughter the night before.

He gave directions but didn't reveal our destination. The streetlights came on and made haloes in the darkening evening around us. First Mannerheimintie, then Vihdintie — we were headed out of town. I reminded myself again why I was here, why I had agreed to this. I wanted revenge, a balanced account. I didn't want anyone else meddling any more. This was my vengeance, my task to perform. I wanted to get clarity, to get Henrik Saarinen for what he'd done, whatever it was. I wanted to stop him from doing what he was planning to do, what I sensed was about to happen.

"Aleksi."

I glanced at him. He looked as if he'd been painfully struck somewhere on his body. His breathing was shallow, his body tense, his face expectant.

"Do you feel as if you're close?" he asked, and didn't wait for an answer. "I know how it feels to be close. To be so close that it feels as if what you want most is no more than an arm's length away. That the only thing you have to do is hold out a few more moments and then all you need is to accept your share, receive what justly belongs to you. With a big smile, your face glowing, your hands held out. And inside, a certainty that this is what will happen, what is supposed to happen, what was supposed to happen. That the universe has finally adjusted itself a few millimetres in the right direction, even though it hasn't."

He shot me a quick glance.

"Aleksi, I know who you are."

I kept my hands on the steering wheel.

"It's all right," he said. "I forgive you. Your intentions have been good, and we have the same goal."

How quickly could I get my seatbelt open, get my hand on something? Saarinen was agile and quick for his age and size.

"Stay on this road, Aleksi Kivi."

I looked in the rearview mirror. We would stay on this road.

"Do you know what separates expectation from fulfilment?" he asked.

I shook my head.

"You've waited for years," he said, his voice a mix of sincerity and exaggerated surprise. "You know something about that. And I do, too. I've learned to like the waiting. It makes a person do his best, reach his potential. The tougher, the more challenging it is to wait, the more ready you become. Waiting makes us vigilant, attunes us, prepares us for what we have to do in order for the waiting to end one day." He licked his lips as if he'd just eaten. "Waiting has its good side. You can imagine the fulfilment of your desire. The more deliciously you build it up, the more you put into it, the more enjoyable the waiting becomes. I'm sure you feel the same way."

"And what about fulfilment?" I asked. "You must have experience with that, too."

I could feel his gaze on my cheek, my temple. My foot was still on the accelerator. I was obeying the speed limit.

"In many ways," Saarinen said.

We crossed the third ring road and kept going. I could hear Saarinen's breathing beside me, shallow and tremulous. Minutes passed. The dark autumn woods crowded closer towards the road on either side.

"We'll turn left about half a kilometre ahead," Saarinen said.

If he hadn't warned me I would have driven past it. It was a narrow opening in the black wall of forest leading to a small gravel road. The headlights swept over tree trunks and undergrowth. At the end of the road a lone outdoor light shone. Several hundred metres on we came to an ordinary sixties or seventies-era building, a combination of a house and some kind of garage. The building was dark except for an outdoor light on the brick wall. The road seemed to lead straight towards the house, but it veered left at the last moment and continued up a steep incline behind the building. Motion detectors lit up the yard with two bright lights.

I stopped the car. The house seemed fairly well-kept. The windows were dark. I turned off the engine at Saarinen's request and we got out. The evening chill went straight for my bare neck and fingers. It was so quiet that our steps on the gravel and the tiled porch sounded as if they'd been fed through a loudspeaker. When we got to the door at the back of the house Saarinen waved me aside, turned the lock, and beckoned me in.

The air was musty and mildewy. I put my hand on the light switch and said, "Shall I?"

"Of course," Saarinen said. "We're here for a good cause."

I turned on the lights. At the same second, Saaarinen reached for something on a table in the corner. He unwound a cord. The nail gun. The one we bought. The movement itself frightened me. The same trajectory that I'd recognised, or thought I recognised, a long time ago.

A dim hallway stretched ahead of us into the house. On the right was a living room, on the left a kitchen. There were only a few pieces of furniture. It looked as if no one lived there. I didn't have to ask who owned the house. Saarinen did, no doubt, or more likely one of his companies.

"The end of the hall," I heard him say behind me.

The darkness wasn't inviting, but I was in an abandoned house with a man holding a nail gun behind me. I took a few wary steps and saw that there was an empty shelf at the end of the hall with a closed white door on either side of it. The only difference between the doors was that one had two locks. The upper one was a padlock, new and shiny. The door looked as if it were reinforced as well. I heard Saarinen rummaging in the pocket of his leather jacket.

"Here," he said, and handed me a ring with three keys on it. "It's only fitting that you should open the door."

I took the keys and found the right one on the first try. The padlock was heavy in my hand, foreboding. It didn't offer safety. I put it on the empty shelf. I opened the door and took a breath. What was I thinking about? Surprisingly simple things — the door opening; the couple of metres between me and Saarinen with the nail gun; the flood of stuffy air from the room behind the door, a mix of sour human exhalation, nights spent in a too small space, and other body odours — sweat, urine, fear, waiting; and the house's own unlived-in smell of mildew, damp, and mould.

The room was pitch dark. If there was a window, it was tightly covered.

"The light switch is on the right," Saarinen said.

I fumbled on the wall and turned it on. The light was agonisingly bright, an unshaded bulb, and there was no furniture in the room except for one old wine-red fake leather armchair. In the chair, tied with a variety of ropes and shackles was an old, obstinate, retired — or forcibly retired — former police detective. Ketomaa. His mouth was taped and his eyes blinded by the sudden light. His head flinched, his eyes strained, trying to see in the change from cellar dark to dentist's chair bright.

The former bedroom had been made into a cell. The window was boarded over. The walls were covered in sheets of grey soundproofing. The location of the house hardly made this necessary. The floor was original, spinach-green vinyl.

"All the way in, Aleksi."

I took three short steps. The room was about twenty-five metres square. Ketomaa sat in the chair near the farthest wall. He was trying to say something. I couldn't make out the words; the tape barely let him get any air even through his nostrils. I heard Saarinen's steps behind me, then beside me. He chose his position strategically. He was between me and the door, an equal distance from me and from Ketomaa. My muscles were trembling. What had I expected? Not this, anyway.

"Are you ready to take the next step?" Saarinen asked.

Ketomaa stopped moving. He tried again to open his eyes. I didn't know what to say. Or what to say first.

"Are you going to put down that nail gun?"

I looked at Saarinen and then at the hardware store bag lying on the floor. There was a knife in it, at least.

Saarinen didn't seem to hear my question. Instead he slipped out of his coat one sleeve at a time, switching the nail gun from his right to his left hand and back again in a quick, rhythmic dance. Finally he hung the coat on the door handle. He looked at Ketomaa.

"And tell me where this is going?" I said.

He seemed to be able to hear me again.

"This man," he said, waving the nail gun in a wide arc at Ketomaa's head, "has been meddling in my affairs for twenty years."

"For no reason?"

Ketomaa blinked, shaking his head back and forth again. He recognised our voices. I turned to look at Saarinen. He looked at me. I don't think I was too far off when I thought that we were finally seeing each other.

"What do you mean?" Saarinen said.

"Put down the nail gun and we'll talk," I said.

He did the opposite of what I asked. He gripped the gun tighter.

"Aleksi. I don't understand. This is what's best for you and Amanda, it's for your sake."

I didn't know what he was talking about. He seemed to be surprised and angry. His posture straightened. He pulled his shoulders back as far as they would go. For the first time all evening I felt pure, undiluted fear.

"I've made an investment in you," Saarinen said quietly. Though he was talking to me, his eyes were on Ketomaa.

A large man with a nail gun in his hand. A man tied to a chair. A room with a lock.

"Amanda," I said. "You just said something about her and me, about what's best for us."

Anything to defuse the situation, ease it enough to give me time to think of my next move. I saw three possibilities: the light switch, a knife, maybe a hammer, in the bag, or a direct attack. That was the least tempting. I could almost feel the nails sink into my flesh, my muscle, my stomach, which was aching with tension.

Saarinen seemed to be thinking. That was new, too. The big man was unsure. Ketomaa had got his eyes open. He answered my gaze with surprising calm.

"Can I depend on you?" Saarinen asked.

"Of course," I said as quickly and reassuringly as I could. "It's just that this has come . . . sort of out of the blue."

"This is all new to you, of course," Saarinen said, as if we were talking about taking up a new hobby. "To both of us. A new, bewildering situation. I'm sure you remember when I said that I saw something more than a handyman in you."

I nodded. I noticed that Ketomaa kept his eyes entirely on me. He didn't seem to be interested in Saarinen at all.

"I see a man who would make a perfect husband for Amanda. The kind of man she needs. Someone with his feet on the ground. Someone who can make her give up . . . make her stop . . ."

I remembered Amanda's eye swollen shut, her lip ripped open. Every idea, every word I could think of to say was wrong. I couldn't rattle Saarinen. He was between me and the door, as well as the light switch.

"What about Amanda? Does she know about this?"

Saarinen looked at Ketomaa.

"No," he said. "And she can't know. That's why it's important that we find some solution when it comes to Ketomaa."

"What do you mean?"

"I tried to talk to him," Saarinen said, as if Ketomaa weren't right in front of him but somewhere far away. "I tried to explain to him how damaging it would be if he kept up his pestering, spreading lies. And I'm not just talking about myself. I'm used to his annoyances, used to him pestering me with his ridiculous accusations, but this affects other people, too."

"Don't you think you should try again to talk to him? Wouldn't that be a better option than this?"

Ketomaa's eyes stayed locked on me. His demeanour was calm, dignified. He seemed to approve of my play for time. On the other hand, he didn't have much choice, under the circumstances. Saarinen didn't answer right away. I looked at him. Would it be possible to knock him down before I got half a dozen nails in my face?

"I tried. I tried all the way here to convince him that he was wrong about me, once and for all. That he had nothing to gain by spreading his lies, that he was only hurting people. Then we got here. We had a bit of a confrontation. He's quick for an old man. I got a chisel through my hand."

He lifted his bandaged hand as if in salute. With the nail gun in his other hand he looked like a member of some militant sect.

"In my opinion we have just one choice," he said, bringing the nail gun closer to Ketomaa's head.

"Wait a minute," I said.

"Aleksi, you have a wonderful future ahead of you. The only thing you have to do is help me with this."

I took a breath. The nail gun was pressed against Ketomaa's temple.

"I want to ask you something," I said.

Saarinen looked at me. He didn't look uncertain or angry any more. He looked kind. I didn't know what was more frightening, the steel nails, now aimed at my head from ten centimetres away, or the warm half smile, also aimed at me, filled with fatherly approval.

"Of course," he said quietly.

"If Ketomaa has been after you for twenty years, there must be some reason."

"Aleksi, if you knew detective Ketomaa you would know that he is an obsessive, deluded person, and the longer he dwells on something the more convinced he is that he's in the right."

"Twenty years ago . . ."

"I lost someone I loved, but I had nothing to do with it."

Saarinen looked at me. I wasn't sure what passed between us. He tilted his head.

"Can we get started?"

"No," I said. It was the first, the most natural word that occurred to me.

"No? Aleksi, you can change your whole life tonight. Your whole life. I know how you covet Amanda, how much you want her."

Did I? Did I want her? Why had the idea even occurred to me? Why was everything so complicated? Why was nothing clear? Even my certainty of Henrik Saarinen's guilt was gone, just when it would have been most useful to me.

"This is your chance," Saarinen said. "I need your help, but not until later. If you don't want to watch the action, you can close your eyes."

"How about I turn off the light?" I said, ignoring the conflicting thoughts struggling in my mind.

"All right," Saarinen said, patiently, as if he was on his best behaviour, talking to a troubled friend. "The nails will hit their mark just as well in the dark."

I took a step towards the switch and made my decision. At the same second, Saarinen realised what I was doing.

"I can turn them off —"

His sentence was interrupted.

I sprang forward, struck his side with my shoulder. I took him down with me and tried to reach the hand that held the nail gun. We hit the wall to the right of Ketomaa and fell on the floor, my legs trapped under him. I tried to stop his hand.

It was too late.

I heard the nail gun fire at least three times. Ketomaa let out an animal sound. Saarinen turned quickly, trying to stand up, was able to rise almost to his full height. I got hold of his shoulder and managed to trip him. He started to fall. I threw myself at his back with all my weight. He made it to the door. He either fell against the light switch or turned it off on purpose. The room went dark.

Through the crack of the door, from down the long hallway, a weak glimmer of yellow light shone. Saarinen fell on the floor. Again I was unable to get a firm grip on the large man.

The gun spat out nails.

One, two, three, four, five.

Some of them hit Ketomaa. I got hold of Saarinen's hand and aimed the gun at the ceiling. I lunged forward on all fours. I was a little too fast, went past my target, but I hit his chin with my knee. The nail gun skidded across the floor into the shadows somewhere in the corner of the room. I struggled after it.

Saarinen spun in the other direction, stood up, swung back, and kicked me in the stomach. The pain was paralysing. I slid my hands over the dark floor, looking for the gun. Saarinen kicked me again. Could he see where the tool he'd made his weapon was?

"Aleksi," he said in a breathless voice. "This. Is. A disappointment."

A weak, narrow beam of light came from behind him.

"If you (kick) Only knew (kick) What I've done (kick) For you (kick)."

I tried to get away. I'd lost my sense of direction. The light was growing even dimmer, or I was starting to lose consciousness. It was impossible to breathe. The attempt no longer seemed worth the oxygen. The vinyl floor beneath my hands was rocking like the open sea.

Finally my hand touched something. It seemed too good to be true. I couldn't understand why Saarinen wasn't trying to get hold of the nail gun. I took one more kick, in the leg. I wrapped my fingers around the handle of the gun and rolled onto my back. I aimed at the ray of light.

It seemed Saarinen hadn't thought I would make it that far. I saw a darkness flash in front of the beam of light, then the door opening and the shape of a man against the doorway. I fired nails towards the door and heard them hit the wall. I got up onto my knees.

Saarinen took a few running steps. I scrambled to my feet and made it to the doorway. I leaned on the handle and let the nails fly down the hallway. I heard a car start. I saw lights outside as I stumbled against the walls all the way to the back door.

I came to the yard and saw the Land Cruiser pull away. I took a breath and the cool autumn air filled my lungs and cleared my head. Then I went back to the room and turned on the lights, afraid of what I would see.

The nails had hit Ketomaa in the chest and face. His head was flopped back, his face shining red with blood. He looked dead. I got the knife from the hardware bag, went over to him, lifted his head carefully, and listened. I thought I could hear a weak, barely perceptible breath from his nostrils. I let his blood-wet head rest against my stomach, and took firm hold of his face. I could feel one of the nails in his cheek, long and firm and unyielding against my hand. I put the knife against the side of his mouth.

The tape wouldn't break. There was blood coming out everywhere, making it hard to hold onto his face, his skin sticky and slippery. I pulled the tape off. His chin dropped and I heard him breathing. I took a step towards the door, went through Saarinen's coat pockets, and found a mobile phone. It was the most basic of models, the cheapest you can buy. A strange choice for a man with expensive tastes.

I called the emergency number, told them there'd been a work accident, and didn't stay on the line although they asked me to.

I turned off the phone, wiped it, and threw it in the corner.

My thoughts were confused, as were the words I said to the old man. I cut him free from the chair and laid him on the cold floor. He was unconscious, limp and covered in dark blood. He was thinner than I remembered. He felt as if he didn't weigh enough to produce the pool of blood that surrounded us as I knelt down beside him and heard an ambulance siren.

The woods were dark. I ran hard. My shoes were wet and cold, my trousers covered in dirt and blood. The woods went on further than I'd thought.

When I'd heard the ambulance approaching I'd pressed my ear close to Ketomaa's mouth and heard him breathing. Then I stood up and waited for the ambulance to come around the house and stop at the back door, which I'd left open. I went down the stairs to the ground floor, opened the front door and left, walking along the side of the house into the nearby, dense forest.

I knew I was taking a big risk. If Ketomaa couldn't tell the authorities what had happened at the house, I would be a suspect; there were traces of me everywhere, especially on the nail gun, where they would probably find a print from every one of my fingers. Not to mention DNA. But Ketomaa had been alive when I left. He would tell them about Saarinen, about his kidnapping, about Saarinen's plans. And Saarinen — I had to find him.

What other choice did I have? As I watched the flashing blue lights approaching I realised that I would be in jail in half an hour if I stayed where I was. There were only two people in the house, a badly injured, unconscious victim, and me, with the weapon in my hand. Who would believe even for a minute a story about how the millionaire Henrik Saarinen wanted me to marry his daughter and this was his way of making it happen? No one, at least not until Saarinen's presence there could be proved, and that might take weeks. When I stood up, my knees wet with blood, I decided that if I had to spend time in jail I would do it after I'd seen Saarinen face to face.

I went around the residential areas, keeping clear of outdoor lights. Finally I found what I was looking for. I crossed a ditch next to a yard, checking the lighted windows to make sure no one was looking out. I ran to the clothesline and tore down some men's jeans and a sweatshirt, then ran back into the woods. I shoved the clothes under my coat, to keep them clean, and kept running for a quarter of an hour. I came to a larger road and saw a bus stop in the distance, and people waiting there. Hidden by some bushes, I took off the bloody trousers and shirt and put on a strange man's large jeans, clammy with damp, and the dark blue sweatshirt with a Lions Club logo on the right breast. I emptied my own pockets and shoved my wallet and phone into the pockets of the baggy, clumsily rolled-up jeans. The sweatshirt felt like a sackful of wet dishrags. I pulled on my coat and walked to the bus stop.

When the bus came, I saw that it was headed to Kamppi shopping centre, in central Helsinki. That suited me. I paid the fare with my bank card, adding one more piece of evidence to the growing pile that would eventually topple on me. I sat in the first empty pair of seats. I was damp through. The cold had sunk deep into my bones. My teeth wanted to chatter. I tried to keep them still. I hoped that the weak warmth of the bus would reach me eventually. I couldn't hear any sirens. That didn't mean anything. The area was probably crawling with police cars. The paramedics had no doubt called the police in as soon as they saw that it wasn't the DIY accident I'd reported when I called. The call — that was another piece of evidence against me. I'd lost count of all the suspicious things I'd done in the past hour. I sat in my stolen clothes trying to warm up and thinking about what to do next.

The bus wound its way through neighbourhoods I knew only by name. One by one they were left behind. We reached Helsinki city limits. Saarinen's words were taking on more and more new meanings as I thought about them.

I see a man who would make a perfect husband for Amanda. The kind of man she needs. Someone with his feet on the ground. Someone who can make her give up . . . make her stop . . .

Aleksi, you have a wonderful future ahead of you. The only thing you have to do is help me with this.

I lost someone I loved, but I had nothing to do with it.

If you only knew what I've done for you.

The bus arrived at Kamppi. I decided to get on another one. I would go back to Kalmela. Start there. But before that I would need something to eat, or at least something to drink. My stomach ached, my throat was rough and dry.

I went up the escalator to the shopping centre and knew all at once that I was the loneliest person on earth. I didn't even want to think about what I looked like in my wet, mud-soaked shoes, my too-big, uncle-style jeans, and my Lions Club sweatshirt, stuffed up under my coat. I didn't know how dirty my face was, how messy my hair was. I had tried to see my reflection in the bus window, afraid Ketomaa's blood had got onto my cheek, my chin, my forehead, wiping my nose and mouth with my sleeve and finger-combing my hair into what I imagined was a presentable state.

The loud bustle of the shopping centre told me the shops were about to close. I was just in time. I walked into a grocery store without looking around me. I saw couples shopping together, their happiness, their clean clothes.

I found a shelf of sandwiches, grabbed one with chicken and a bottle of cola. If I ran I could still make the next bus to Kalmela. I turned towards the cashier's counter, stopped, froze, and my jaw would have dropped all the way to my wet, miserable feet if the dried sweat and dirt on my cheeks weren't holding it up.

When had we last seen each other? Was it only six weeks ago?

I couldn't form words. All I could do was stare.

What thoughts can you have in a hundredth of a second? How much regret? How many things can you realise you've done wrong, how many ways you've been a fool?

Miia's expression changed from second to second, like a sleek, quick elevator moving from one floor to the next.

First surprise, a half happy look, then just plain surprise, open bewilderment, and finally shock, sympathy, shame. Obviously I looked even worse than I'd feared. She glanced to the side, into the next aisle, then looked at me again. She was dressed in a black, knee-length jacket, red jeans, and a patterned scarf.

"Hello, Aleksi."

"Hi," I said, making myself speak. I couldn't find the words. "How have you been? Out grocery shopping?"

Brilliant, I thought. At the same moment I saw what was in her basket. Cheese, fruit, fish, bread. Maybe going to a friend's. Or maybe friends were coming to

226

her house. I remembered long evenings in her lovely home. Another time. Another world.

"Sort of. We're . . . buying some dinner. I've been well. Thanks for asking."

"That's good to hear," I said, holding a limp, ready-made sandwich and a tepid, sugary drink in my hands. Next to the Gouda, Manchego, and Brie, gravlax and rye bread in her basket it looked more like punishment than food.

"How're things with you?" she asked.

"Very good," I said. "Just grabbing a snack before I hop on the bus."

She looked at me. I felt her gaze traverse from my head to my toes and back again. She waved her free hand, as if to help me see my condition.

"Was this your big secret? You were planning to become a wino?"

I shook my head.

"I haven't become a wino."

"What, then?"

I shifted my feet into a firmer stance. My wet shoes squished out water. Glancing down I saw that my sweatshirt reached nearly to my knees, like an ugly skirt. And I couldn't take it off — the shirt underneath was stained with blood.

"This isn't how it looks," I said, and congratulated myself again. Where were these banalities coming from?

"No doubt. What bus?"

"What?"

"You're grabbing a snack before you hop on a bus. That's what you said, anyway. But then you say all kinds of things and make people believe all kinds of things. Where is this bus going?"

I realised that the people in the store were giving me more space than they normally did. It was possible that I reeked of sweat, dirt, and wet clothes. I felt like yelling to Miia and everyone else to just try to keep from sweating when somebody's shooting at you with a nail gun and kicking you in the stomach and ribs and you have to run from the police through the dark woods and you've hoped and feared for twenty years and wanted justice for the mother who was taken away from the little boy you once were.

"Going to work," I said quietly.

"So you are working."

"Of course."

"You look like you . . . Like you're not working. Where are you working?"

"I can't tell you."

Miia had the same familiar look in her eye that I'd seen on that horrible night when every word tore a little more of my heart away.

"Of course you can't. I forgot you work for the CIA. Aleksi, are you living on the street?"

I was so tired that I didn't have it in me to deny it, or to try to explain somehow, from another angle.

"Miia, could I call you some —"

Before I could finish my question a thirtyish, well-dressed man appeared from between the grocery shelves. He placed himself next to Miia. He was of average build, with an elegant, striped tie, knotted with studied carelessness, dark-rimmed glasses, and dimples in his cheeks that deepened with a quick, practised expression.

"This is Olli," Miia said, glancing at him. "And this is Aleksi."

Olli demonstrated that he was a civilised man in matters other than just dress. He reached out to shake my hand. I did the same. At the very end of the reach, just before our hands clasped, he hesitated. He'd seen my hand. I saw it too, for the first time. It must have been because of the bright, cold light in the supermarket. My hand looked as if it had been digging through guts and then done some gardening. Which it had, in a way. Our hands clasped. Olli took back his hand and left it hanging away from his body.

"I've heard about you," he said.

Miia coughed into her fist.

"Heard good things," Olli added.

"I'm sure," I said.

His eyes did the same thing Miia's had just done, moving from my muddy shoes to my dirty forehead and back. They couldn't get enough of me. I was like an object lesson in failure, a loser, a bizarre relic, the lunatic exception in her otherwise sensible past.

"We should go," Miia said. "Take care."

"OK. You, too," I said, to no one in particular.

Of course I'd heard that old saying about how before you die your whole life flashes before your eyes. It did. I watched Miia's retreating back, her hand reaching for Olli's upper arm, the brisk movement of her boots, and I felt as if I was dying.

SEPTEMBER 2013

Kalmela was deserted. I knew as soon as I saw the main house that Henrik Saarinen wasn't there, so my trip was partly in vain.

The night wind kept a steady hum through the trees, otherwise everything was still, with no sign of life. The windows of the manor house were black as the mouth of a tunnel. The wan glow of the yard lights made the house seem separate from its surroundings, as if it could get up and leave. I'd walked four kilometres in the dark along the road and thought way too much. I wanted a warm shower, longed for dry, clean clothes so much that it hurt.

Common sense told me I had time. It would be a while before I could talk to Ketomaa. My fingerprints weren't in any registry, nor was my DNA. They would only know I had been there if Ketomaa told them, and I didn't think he would. I didn't know what Saarinen was guilty of besides what he'd done to Ketomaa, but I was fairly certain he wouldn't be the first one to turn himself in.

The main house was quieter than ever. I made a quick circuit of the inside although I knew deep down that there was no point. I stopped in the middle of the hall. Suddenly everything seemed such a long time ago. The day I came to the estate, meeting Amanda and Henrik, doing my maintenance work. Back when I knew what I was doing. That thought took me in its fist and squeezed. The night grew darker. I was shivering with cold. I turned out the lights and went to my apartment.

I undressed, stuffed the clothes I was wearing in a rubbish bag, and tied it closed. I shoved the bag under a cabinet, not for a moment believing that what was out of sight would be out of mind. I was under the hot shower for a long time, used quantities of shampoo and soap. Ketomaa's blood rinsed down the drain, but the guilt for my old friend's suffering didn't come off as easily. I told myself over and over that I'd done what I could, acted on the understanding I'd had, and that I would help him in every way possible.

After my shower I toasted some rye bread, spread some of Enni's elk pâté on it, and ate it with a mug of coffee. I thought many times of calling Amanda, but something stopped me — maybe what Saarinen had said, maybe just a desire to have at least a little time and distance from what had happened.

As I ate I stared blindly out of the window. The main house was still there, shining in the night like a ship, mute and self-assured. If it was keeping secrets it wasn't going to tell them. Coming here hadn't been like opening a treasure chest or rolling a stone from the mouth of a cave the way I'd thought it would be, but

I'd come, and now I was here, and everything that had happened had happened for a reason.

Ketomaa had believed Saarinen was guilty. I had believed Saarinen was guilty. Saarinen had thought Ketomaa's investigation was harassment. And he had let me get close to him.

I turned out the lights and lay down on the bed. Slowly but surely the darkness took on shapes, outlines.

Early the next morning, a little before seven, I walked to the bus stop again. The sun was just starting its rise, its light dawning a delicate pink on the horizon. I waited for the bus next to the dark, impenetrable spruce forest, going through my phone files with fingers stiff from the morning cold. I was looking for a number I could call. There weren't any. I searched through yesterday's evening news for a headline or even a mention of the incident or of Ketomaa, but I didn't find anything. I couldn't call the Meilahti hospital, where I assumed Ketomaa had been taken. They wouldn't release information to a stranger.

The bus came into view. I waved an arm to get it to stop. There weren't many passengers, and the trip into Helsinki went quickly. I sat in the second row of seats and watched the sunrise change from pink to red to autumn yellow as it climbed the sky and eventually shone into my eyes.

I walked from the Kamppi terminal to Liisankatu. My car was where I'd left it, with an 80 euro parking ticket under the wiper. I shoved the ticket in my coat pocket. I started the car and was about to drive away, then didn't. I locked the car again and walked the short distance to Amanda's building. I rang the bell and waited. No answer. Perhaps it was too early. I didn't see Amanda's black SUV anywhere. I wanted to talk to her, ask her where I could find Henrik. Talking on the phone wasn't the same, especially not now. I went back to my car and waited to see if I could get another parking fine. Two hours later I went to a café down the street and ordered a croissant and a cup of coffee. I went to the little WC and looked at myself in the mirror. I looked better than I had when I ran into Miia the night before. Which was no consolation. The thought of Miia was painful and bleak.

In the afternoon I moved the car for something to do. I found another no parking zone a little way down the street. Young people were pouring out of a school, fourteen- to seventeen-year-olds, alone or in larger groups. I remembered my loneliness at that age, my constant awareness that I would never walk home like that again, that nothing would ever be like it was before.

That feeling had always been with me. I couldn't shake it on the football field, at the cinema, with girls or later women, alone, no matter when or where. Maybe that was why I developed two separate lives, one inside and one outside. Inside I was searching for the truth, carrying out a task, the same task whose outcome I was waiting for now as I sat in the car. On the outside I did all the things that other people my age were doing: school, sports, studying, working. Maybe I should congratulate myself. The moment had come when those two hopelessly separate lives seemed finally to be merging.

Life had never been what I'd once thought it would be. Nothing had happened the way I had imagined it would. The only certainties were the vanishing days, and the unknowability of those to come.

A little before four o'clock I looked up. Amanda Saarinen's black Range Rover appeared in my wing mirror. It rolled up from the direction of the shore like a wagon into a new city, swaying over the cobblestone street, slowly advancing as if its driver were exceedingly on guard. It wasn't a style of driving that matched Amanda's personality. The black side of the SUV passed me and found a parking spot almost directly in front of Amanda's building, on the opposite side of the street. It seemed Amanda really did get whatever she wanted. I couldn't begin to imagine how that felt.

I got out of the car and noticed that my legs were stiff as I hurriedly crossed the street. Amanda was sitting in her car wearing sunglasses. I went to the building entrance. I let the seconds, then the minutes, pass. Finally she opened the car door, climbed out, and saw me. I could tell because her back stiffened and she glanced quickly around her, the way a person does when she has to encounter someone she doesn't want to encounter, or so I imagined.

She was dressed entirely in black, which made her look thinner. Her knee-length black leather coat was narrow and tight-fitting, as were her black blouse, black trousers, and black leather boots. Her face and neck were paler than I remembered. Her lip was swollen and slightly purple.

"Have you been waiting long?" she asked.

I couldn't see her eyes behind her sunglasses. Judging by her voice, the question was a rhetorical one.

"There are a couple of things we need to talk about," I said.

"As it happens, I was thinking the same thing."

She rattled the bundle of keys in her hand and pushed one into the door lock. I followed her up. I walked behind her, as I had before, but I didn't feel the same sense of expectation as I had then. Nothing like it. And I didn't know why. Of course there were the events of the night before — her father shooting nails at people, and running away as I shot them at him. But that didn't totally explain it.

Amanda didn't take off her tall boots, instead wore them into the apartment, into the kitchen, took a bottle of white wine from the refrigerator, poured herself a glass, and walked with it in her hand into the living room, where she sat down on the sofa. She was still wearing the sunglasses. I sat in the chair across from her. The afternoon sun was trying to penetrate the recessed window, making dim, long shadows that would disappear in a brief moment.

"Fuck, what a night. And day."

I couldn't have said it better myself. Amanda took off her sunglasses. The black eye was purple now.

"First I'm woken up in the middle of the night and they refuse to tell me what's happened —"

"Who woke you up?" I asked.

"The police."

I looked at her. She took a sip of wine. I decided not to interrupt her again, to listen first to what she had to say. Then I would tell her what had happened to me. Or would I? I lowered my hands onto the armrests and waited. She held the glass of wine in front of her face, looking over it at the darkened room.

"This thing between us is over, by the way," she said, as if she was making a passing remark about the weather.

I'd decided not to interrupt. I was also thinking about Miia, about my misery when I saw her. Amanda's words seemed to fall by the wayside.

"Where was I?" she said. "Right. They woke me up, asked to come in, and asked me all kinds of strange questions. When had I last seen my father? Had he said anything that struck me as suspicious? Things like that. And they wouldn't tell me what it was about, although it was clear something had happened."

A swallow of wine.

"A couple of hours of that, and then they started to hint to me that my father had tried to kill somebody. I showed them this." She sighed and pointed at her eye, in case I didn't know what she meant. "I said that's what he could accomplish when he wasn't even trying to kill anybody. Then they asked me what I knew about Enni Salkola."

The glass emptied. She seemed to be considering whether to fill it again or keep talking.

"I told them all I knew was that she'd been cooking for my dad for a long time. They asked me whether I thought Henrik had any reason to murder Enni. I said of course not, unless you counted a slightly overdone creme brûlée."

She looked at me.

"Then they said that he tried to kill her last night."

I struggled to put the events, the people, together in my mind, but I couldn't manage it no matter how I tried. I sat quiet, waiting for her to continue. Her story wasn't what I'd expected. Nothing was.

"Aleksi."

I raised my head.

"Why are you here?"

I shook my head.

"No reason," I said.

Amanda looked at me, expressionless, her eyes cool and hard. Why was it that at moments like this my mind brought up things that I usually was able to keep out of sight, under the surface? I thought about my mother. I went over and over what had happened at the abandoned house, what Saarinen had said. I knew I should tell Miia everything. No matter what her reaction was.

"Do you know anything about this?" Amanda asked, leaning forward and resting her thin elbows on her thin knees. She looked like a scorpion. "Because I feel really weird right now."

I shook my head again.

"No," I said, as convincingly as I could. "So Henrik tried to kill Enni. Was she badly hurt?"

Amanda looked at me as if I'd broken her favourite vase, done something outrageously crude and bizarre.

"No. Enni was not badly hurt. Enni defended herself. My dad is dead."

The darkness didn't creep into the room, it ran in, flooded in. The world behind Amanda dimmed; the shadows melted together. I realised that I couldn't see her eyes any more. A great, cold wind swept through me.

"I'm sorry," I said.

"For what?"

She lifted her elbows from her knees and leaned back again. A woman in black in a dark room, like a painting from a couple of hundred years ago. Like a bad dream.

"Sorry that your father . . . that he's dead."

"Wasn't that the idea?"

I didn't answer. Amanda ran her fingers through her hair. Henrik Saarinen was dead. It was over. Twenty years, and now it was over. The thought didn't fit into the world.

"Don't pretend you hadn't thought about it," Amanda said. "About what would come after. Once Amanda's father is out of the picture and you get Amanda and all her money."

"I'm not interested in . . ."

She lifted her shoulders, set her head at the appropriate angle.

"A flat-broke carpenter," she said in a cold, hard voice. "Grew up in Vallila. Used to run a second-hand bookshop. Jumping into bed with an heiress. Of course you weren't thinking about money."

I couldn't see even her face now, and I didn't need to. I remembered when we met, what we'd said, what had happened, how one thing led to another. It was all absurdly logical. There was no point in claiming that I was surprised. I knew my weaknesses. I knew what would happen if I gave them even half a chance.

"Now I really think you should leave," Amanda said. "I'm expecting someone."

OCTOBER 2013

Over the next two weeks the police brought me in for questioning twice. I also received a request from Elias Ahlberg, Henrik Saarinen's lawyer, to continue working at Kalmela until notified otherwise.

During the police interviews I answered only the questions directed at me. I didn't offer anything about my own experiences or theories. No one had connected me with the events in the abandoned house, for the time being, and Ketomaa wasn't going to either — he was being kept in a coma, for medical reasons. And contrary to what I'd expected, Mansikka-aho hadn't got in touch with me at all.

Piece by piece I put together a basic picture of what had happened between Henrik and Enni.

Henrik had arrived disoriented at Enni's apartment at Kalmela. He told her he'd been the innocent victim of an assault and that he couldn't go to the police. He didn't tell her what had happened or where he had been. He insisted that she hide him until he could decide what to do. He had dried blood on his shirt cuffs. Enni was frightened. She wanted to call the police. Henrik firmly forbade it. She tried anyway. He knocked the phone out of her hand. She tried to get out of the apartment. Henrik attacked her. She had bruises on her upper arm and wrist. Henrik backed off. Enni ran into the kitchen to make the call from there. Henrik followed her. She was panicked. He was yelling things that she didn't understand. She feared she was going to die. He raised his fist and lunged at her. She grabbed a knife. He stopped. The long, steel knife had gone through his aorta and his heart muscle. He died immediately.

Enni was released after a short time. She hadn't come back to work, and I hadn't seen her anywhere around the estate.

I hadn't seen Amanda either. I hadn't even heard from her. I noticed that the thought of her gave me goosebumps, made me afraid she would turn up, surprise me from behind. Whenever I thought about her I started looking around. The shadows took on her shape, variations in the landscape, noises from the next room seemed like signs that she was somewhere nearby.

I felt as if I was floating, in spite of the fact that my days were long and filled with work. When I didn't have any real work to do, I invented something. I particularly liked being on the shore, repairing the dock or the sauna. The first week of October was unusually dry. The days were clear and blue, full of cool, clean air and gentle breezes. The sun tried its best to rise, but every day its reach was a tiny bit lower than the day before. In the mornings it mixed its palette of reds and violets on the horizon, painted broad streaks of pink that tore through the black. I worked outside, kept my hands and feet busy — and floated.

Thinking was the same as remembering. Both hurt.

I knew that staying at the estate was making things worse but I wasn't ready to leave yet. Henrik Saarinen had been the reason I came here. Now he was gone. So why didn't I go? What was keeping me there? I didn't know. Saarinen had taken the knowledge of my mother's fate with him, and the knowledge of what he'd meant by what he'd said when Ketomaa was tied to that chair.

The handrail on the dock was a white-painted lattice a metre and a half high and the sea next to it was as hard on the paint as it was on the wood underneath. Replacing it felt like the right kind of busy work. It was a chore that could have been put off for a year, or even two, but I could just as well do it now. I was tearing the railing down when I stopped to stretch my back and looked up at the main building.

Someone had opened the double doors on the veranda; the wind fluttered the white and yellow striped curtains. They waved restlessly in and out and climbed the walls like tongues flicking and licking around a mouth. I watched them for a moment and started towards the house.

The front steps needed sweeping. Leaves blown from the trees were piled thick and matted at the base of each step. Some of them were already grey, some still kept their colour — pale yellow, deep red. The curtains puffed out to meet me as I walked up to the double door. I stepped inside, and stopped.

242

The hall looked different, though the furniture and fixtures were all the same as they'd been that morning. Then I saw what was new: gladioli in a glass vase, their strong, almost intoxicating fragrance. The bouquet was in the same place, the same vase, as when I met Henrik Saarinen for the first time. I heard familiar sounds from the kitchen, cupboard doors opening, a table being set, a glass put down on a wood surface, the clink of metal utensils.

Enni looked the way she'd always looked — absorbed in her work, and slightly surprised to see me. She was wearing white running shoes, loose-fitting dark blue jeans and an apple-green sweater. Her cheeks were flushed, probably from exertion. It was all so normal. It was hard to think about Henrik Saarinen's death, to think that this bustling woman was the person who had dealt it.

"Hi," I said, not wanting to start by expressing my condolences or telling her how sorry I was. I didn't even know if I was sorry. And none of that would have meant anything anyway. The whole thing just was what it was.

"Hi," Enni said, continuing what she was doing, which seemed to be emptying the cupboards and refrigerator. There were grocery bags on the floor, a woven basket on the kitchen table where she was putting jars of her own homemade juice, jam and other delicacies. It seemed to be full. She continued her work for a moment, then looked at me.

"Did Elias talk to you?"

I nodded. "They decided I should stay on until they say otherwise," I said.

"Same for me."

I wasn't going to ask why they would still need a cook in the house when the only regular diner there was dead. It was none of my business.

"Was there something you wanted to ask me?" She'd straightened up to her full height. She was a tall woman, some metre and seventy centimetres tall. She looked straight at me.

"What about?" I asked, although I could guess what she meant.

Her face was friendly. Her red cheeks added to her matronly appearance.

"About what happened. About Henrik."

I shrugged. "I guess not. I'm sure it was . . . unpleasant. Awful, I mean."

"Extremely. But there was nothing else I could do. That's what I've told everyone."

"Of course not."

We stood in silence for a moment. I thought I felt a cold draught on my legs and ankles, the sea air blowing in through the open doors and fluttering curtains.

"I would have been happy to see him remain the master of this house," Enni said. "But he wasn't himself when he came to my apartment. He wasn't Henrik. He was someone else."

People had probably already recommended that she get some kind of crisis treatment or therapy, directed her to someone who could help, listen, prescribe medication. She was talking to me more than she ever

244

had, in a tone she might use to talk about anything at all. At some point I would have to ask her what Henrik had said, whether he had mentioned me, told her what he'd done. She turned her eyes away from me, looked around as if she'd been suddenly shoved into the middle of the kitchen floor.

"I have to finish my work," she said, bending over a plastic bag and taking out an armful of food. "I'm sure you do too. Life goes on. You have to live, eat, do your job. No matter what happens, life goes on. You have no choice in the matter."

I didn't answer. I didn't have anything in particular to say. I was already going out of the door, looking at the autumn light as it poured over the floor, when I heard her voice.

"Aleksi."

She took some glass jars out of the basket, piled them in her arms, and went to the cupboard. She talked as she placed them on the shelves.

"You can get something to eat here this evening. I'll leave some food for you. And go ahead and pick up what you want to take to your apartment."

"Thanks," I said.

"You're welcome," I heard her say from behind the refrigerator door. "It's important that you and I get along. I'm sure that's what Henrik would have wanted, too."

I went back down to the shore and kept working. The sea shone and sparkled calm until sunset, like the top of a lacquered table. When the colours had faded into darkness I gathered up my tools, carried my pack to the sauna, and stood on the porch for a moment. The endless play of the waves on the stones of the shore and the sides of the dock sounded like someone sprinkling pearls from a bag onto a parquet floor. Other sounds, too, were amplified in the darkness. My footsteps as I walked up the path crunched like a hungry man gobbling his food. I had almost forgotten my conversation with Enni but now I remembered it. Or my stomach did.

The main house felt deserted again, as if Enni's visit had never happened. I walked into the kitchen, turned on the lights, and went to the refrigerator. She'd said I could take what I wanted. She had made a meat and cabbage casserole; there was only a sliver missing. She really was doing what she'd said, going on with her life, with making food, even if there was only one person to feed — herself. I found a plate in the cupboard and spooned a generous portion onto it. I was about to put it in the microwave, but decided to eat in my room, at my own table. I could take a few things to put in my refrigerator, too — something for breakfast.

The basket was on the floor. I loaded it with food: gooseberry jam to put in my yogurt, apple juice, winter mushroom salad, and of course some of her elk pâté, rich and meaty, it would go well on a slice of rye toast. I took some other things, too, and set my plate on top of it all. The basket was full and heavy in my hand as I closed the door behind me and walked across the lighted lawn to the outbuilding, climbed the stairs, and went in my apartment.

If I'd sometimes wondered at what solitude was, it became clear to me that evening. Solitude was a deserted estate, dead people, the sound of my own breathing. I did my best to feel like a member of society, of the world. A hot shower, candles on the windowsill, the radio on, a hot meal. The food was steaming and fragrant. The candlelight flickered in a soft puff of air. The light reflected off the window and walls. The cabbage and meat were comforting and filling. Maybe Enni was right. Maybe life would go on.

It took a moment for my mind to register what my eyes were seeing. My gaze went from the vase on the windowsill to the jars on the counter, the inside of the vase, then the jar of pâté. At first I didn't know what had caught my attention. When I realised what it was, I almost spat out my food.

AUGUST 1993

My mother comes in and pulls the door closed behind her. The slam rings in my ears, fading only in steps, as if somewhere far away doors were still slamming. I've come from a football match in Vesa's father's car, and I've already eaten. I'm at the table reading *Lucky Luke*. The Dalton brothers have just escaped from jail when my mother walks into the room. There's only one light source, a lamp with a plastic shade that hangs over the table. She stands at the edge of the pool of light so that I can't see her face. Her black shoes are shining, like they were when she left. She hasn't been walking outside.

How did the match go?

We won 4—2.

Oh, that's nice, she says in a voice that isn't quite the same as when she means what she says. Did it rain the whole time?

Almost.

She takes off her red scarf.

Did you eat all your dinner? she asks.

Almost. So did you have fun?

The red scarf is wrapped around her right hand.

How should I put it? she says. I wouldn't say it was 4—2.

The rain is pouring over the window behind me. What was it I should have said before she left? I can't remember.

What happened? I ask.

She's quiet for a moment.

Do you want to hear?

I nod.

The food was good. The view was pretty. A waterfront restaurant.

Isn't that nice?

It certainly is.

She takes off her coat and puts it on a hanger. She sits on the chair by the front door, takes off her shoes, and pushes them under the chair. Then she straightens up and looks at me. I can see her face.

It's not nice to be dishonest, Aleksi. It's important to be honest. To speak the truth, be who you say you are, and do what you say you're going to do.

She's upset. I realise that. She's doing her best to remain calm, but she's angry, furious. Like she was the time the bathroom upstairs from us started to leak into our bathroom and she had to watch the repairmen to make sure they fixed it the way they should have the first time instead of doing it all wrong and forcing us to move into a spare room at her co-worker's house for two weeks.

She gets up from the chair and comes to the table. I didn't eat my meal. I think I'll have your leftovers.

Why?

Why what?

Why didn't you eat your meal?

She thought for a moment.

Let's not talk about it.

I'm still looking at her. She sighs.

Because of a certain woman, she says, who I wasn't told about and who was very, very unfriendly.

In the restaurant?

She works there.

What did she do to you?

She didn't do anything to me, but I could see what she was doing to the person with me.

Yeah? What?

Her hands stopped. She looked at them, opened and closed her fists, which were smaller than my own.

Something I shouldn't have seen. I just happened to come out of the toilets at that moment.

But what did she do?

You ask an awful lot of questions.

You asked me if I wanted to hear and I said yes.

The same feeling I had had before she left, that something bad was going to happen, has come back. A cold feeling in my stomach, even though it's full of warm macaroni.

What are you going to do? I ask.

She's in our narrow kitchen now, looking in the refrigerator.

Good, there's still some casserole left. I'll go and put on my home clothes and eat.

What are you going to do? I ask again.

She closes the refrigerator, turns, and looks out of the little kitchen window. There's nothing to see but the end of the building next door, dark with rain and yellow from the bottom up to as high as the outside light can reach. My mother straightens her back and puts her hands on the table.

I'm tired of things left unexplained. I intend to get to the bottom of this. I'm going to tell this woman that I want to meet her and I'm going to ask her why she did what she did.

When?

Tomorrow. But not until the evening. And do you know why?

Why?

She turns away from the window and looks at me and smiles and seems like herself again, as if the indignation she felt has flown away with her gaze, slipped out into the rainy, sleeping darkness.

Because we're going to be up so late tonight watching TV and eating popcorn.

It's hard to smile because something cold is banging around in my stomach and it's hard to swallow because my throat feels dry and tight. I try to smile, and when I try really hard, maybe I manage it. My mother puts her hand on my shoulder as she walks past into the bedroom to change her clothes.

I sit for a moment, then get up and go in the kitchen. I look out of the window like she just did.

I don't see anything, but I'm sure that at this moment there's something that I absolutely have to understand, or at least remember.

But I forget it for twenty years. My mother's words. *I'm going to tell this woman that I want to meet her and I'm going to ask her why she did what she did.*

OCTOBER 2013

The humming, rushing sound was coming from inside me. It wasn't the wind in the trees, the gravel under my feet, or the sea far behind me. My steps were long and firm and the late evening was warm and calm considering the time of year.

The little house sat right next to the road, as if it were waiting to be picked up. It was half-lit — the porch and the windows on the right side of the house shone warmly and cast a soft halo over the evening dark. The left side of the house seemed to be asleep. It was completely dark, as if it were part of a different building. I stopped, took a deep breath, and felt in my pocket.

Twenty years.

I walked up the porch steps to the front door and pressed the white button on the frame. There was a high-pitched noise inside. I heard footsteps, and the door opened a crack. After a moment it opened all the way and the warm light flooded out into the October night.

"Aleksi. I've been expecting you."

Evening tea and light brown cookies were laid out beautifully on a little side table in the living room.

There was also a lamp with a brass base and a dark green glass shade on the table that cast a slightly tinted softness over the room. The table was flanked by two leather armchairs with imposing horseshoe-curved backs and the floor was almost entirely covered by a Persian rug, which I was prepared to assume was genuine. The windowsills overflowed with leafy houseplants, there was a sleek stereo system on a bureau with black speakers on either side playing classical music — Wagner, I guessed. The antique lamp that hung from the ceiling wasn't lit; the light in the room came from the table lamp and two floor lamps with fringed shades reminiscent of old photos or museum displays.

The room was small but pleasant.

I sat in the chair offered and waited for my tea. Steam rose from the cup as if it were struggling to get away. I waited for the other cup to be filled, for the teapot to be set down. I reached in my pocket for the bows, and placed them on the table.

"One is from the year 1993," I said. "The other one is new."

The bows were identical. They lay against the dark wood like the wings of an injured butterfly. I raised my eyes and looked across the table.

"When did you notice?"

"Half an hour ago. The slightly darker one," I said, pointing at it, "I've had for twenty years. This one I found on a jar of pâté earlier this evening."

Enni had turned her head so that I saw her in profile. She held her teacup chest-high.

"And that was enough?"

"Of course not. But it made me remember. Things that happened twenty years ago. Things I'd seen and heard. What you said about Henrik. Where you were working. In a waterfront restaurant. The way you make your own foods and tie them up with bows. Like you did with some baked goods twenty years ago. You were already obsessed with Henrik back then, jealous, the way you still were, right up to the very end. I should have realised it the first time I met you, but I was focused on Henrik. I always suspected him, didn't think to look beside him, or under his feet, where you were."

My voice sounded so calm that it didn't seem like my own. I wasn't agitated. More tired than anything.

"My mother was planning to meet you," I said. "She did what she said. She kept her word. My mother wasn't perfect but she kept her word. I'm sure she got in touch with you. I can only guess why it wasn't investigated — she must have called the restaurant and it was somehow misinterpreted. Then she left her office, got into your car, and something happened. It was October, and it was raining, and the whole investigation came too late. So you were able to just drive away, and no one knew where you went."

"Does anyone else know?"

Her voice was neutral, as if she were enquiring about the weather from someone who had a view out of the window.

"No," I said. "I want to know what happened to my mother."

Enni blew on her tea. I couldn't tell if she was smiling or if it was just what her lips did when she blew. The steam trembled.

"Henrik told me," she said, "that you were the missing woman's son."

I didn't say anything. Enni sipped her tea. The muscles of her face twitched. The tea was too hot. The cup went back to its saucer with a clink.

"What do you think of this place?" she asked.

"I'm sorry?"

She turned her head just enough that I could see her whole face. Most of the light was coming from below, and it brought out the recent changes in her appearance. She looked old, her cheeks slightly sunken, the wrinkles around her lips dark and distinct. The biggest change was in her eyes. They were as full of sadness as eyes without tears can be.

"This place," she said, waving a hand.

"Homely."

"Homely," she said. "Twenty-three years, and this is all I get."

I didn't say anything.

"I don't think it's fair. I told Henrik it wasn't fair. I told him again two weeks ago when he came to ask for help, the way he always does when he gets into trouble with other women. And he did get into trouble, for twenty-three years. And I always took him in, comforted him, gave him what he wanted, because he promised. Even now I talk sweetly to him, but like always, he doesn't listen."

256

We sat in silence for a moment. Enni kept her eyes fixed on me. The teacups steamed between us.

"What happened to my mother?" I said.

Enni leaned back in her chair. She looked in front of her, perhaps at the bureau with its speaker sentinels. Wagner thundered and proclaimed.

"Henrik and I were together for some time. We were happy. Or I was, at least. Henrik said he was. I still don't know if it was true. We met when he bought a restaurant on the waterfront where I was working. I wasn't supposed to tell anyone about our relationship. He was always so secretive, you could never talk to anyone about anything. Then along came this woman, your mother."

Enni didn't quite look at me but she turned her head in my direction.

"Henrik grew cold towards me. I couldn't make any contact with him. Do you know how that feels? Of course you do. Amanda must have already done the same thing to you."

She looked at me. The difference, of course, was that I hadn't fallen in love with Amanda. I had just . . . well, what?

"Then they came to have dinner at the very restaurant that had been our place," Enni said. "My heart was broken. Two weeks ago, when Henrik walked in here delirious, his shirt bloody, I realised that I'd buried my resentment for twenty years, but I hadn't forgotten, or forgiven, anything. I told him that. I told him it was over."

She laid her hands in her lap. She took a deep breath in. Then out.

"That evening, twenty years ago, when the woman went to the toilets, I went over to Henrik and told him what he was. Then I slapped him and poured a glass of wine in his lap. I knew that when the woman came back they would leave and Henrik would have to explain what had happened. Your next question will naturally be, why, after all that, Henrik still kept me close to him, or why I wanted to be close to him."

She looked at me, didn't wait for me to ask.

"That's the way love is sometimes. That's how it is when you know things about a person that he doesn't want anyone else to know. Shall I show you?"

Before I could say anything she had taken two quick steps to the bureau, bent down, taken a folder out of the bottom drawer, and handed it to me. I took it, but didn't open it.

"I'm going to ask you again," I said as calmly as I could. "What happened?"

"This pertains to it."

She stood in the middle of the room. I opened the folder.

A photo album. Many photos of Enni when she was younger, as well as Henrik Saarinen. Other people. I easily recognised Enni, Henrik, Amanda, Markus Harmala, at different times, in different clothes, hairstyles, sunglasses. A few group photos. Nothing extraordinary about them, nothing perverse — no leather, or rubber, no animals or eating of faeces. Nothing that you could blackmail someone with. Just people at Kalmela, under the chandeliers, in the summer sunshine, in the boat, eating dinner.

I closed the album and put it on the table.

"I've waited twenty years," I said. "You picked my mother up at work. Then what happened?"

Enni's eyes were averted. She looked like a woman who'd had something taken from her for ever. I knew how that felt.

"We agreed to meet. I drove to her office. She got in the car. We tried to talk. I tried to explain that Henrik belonged to me, but she refused to understand. I raised my hand, maybe too suddenly. Maybe she thought I was going to hit her. She tried to hit me. And I . . . I had a knife with me. For self-defence . . . I brought it from work. I acted instinctively. I don't remember anything. Or not very much. I realised something bad had happened. I panicked. I started the car and drove away."

Enni was a broad-shouldered woman. Compared to her my mother was a featherweight, much too delicate, hopelessly fragile.

"I was acting on instinct," Enni said. "I had been here with Henrik before. I found myself turning onto this road. I'd driven all the way from Helsinki with this woman in the car beside me. It wasn't until I got here that I realised I hadn't been thinking, hadn't considered whether there was anyone here. But the place was deserted and I went to work. I dug a big hole in the woods and buried her. I drove back to Helsinki. I never said a word to anyone about what happened that day. No one asked me. To Henrik I was a wall to talk to, a mattress to have sex on. The police were briefly interested in him, and that was all."

The feeling that was growing inside me wasn't the deep satisfaction of finding out a secret and it wasn't vengeful rage for the wrong done. It was mostly sadness, and a bottomless feeling of loneliness. Enni had taken two or three steps backwards and was leaning against the bureau.

"Did you tell Henrik?" I asked.

"Most of it. I didn't have time . . ."

I lost someone I loved, but I had nothing to do with it.

"That was why he attacked you, wasn't it?"

"I told him I did it for him. He didn't understand."

"Of course he didn't," I said, and finally felt the rage rise inside me. Soon it would fill my head, take over my mind. "You did it for yourself. You were jealous and envious. It wasn't some act of kindness. You took a little boy's mother away from him."

I was standing now. I remembered two things I'd seen that now came together: Enni's skilful use of a knife in the kitchen, and Henrik Saarinen's cause of death. Enni's right hand slipped behind her, into the top drawer of the bureau. I took a step towards her. The hand behind her back darted towards me.

The long knife with its shining blade didn't rise, didn't make any unnecessary motions. It flicked efficiently and purposefully towards my heart. She took a step closer. I did the same. I narrowly avoided getting the knife in my chest but didn't dodge it altogether.

260

The gleaming blade sank into my left arm near the shoulder, went through my coat and polo shirt as if it was bursting a balloon. Enni quickly drew it out again. I looked at her face. Determined. Cold eyes.

I lunged forward. She thrust the knife at me. I took hold of her, forced my left arm to wrap around her throat. The knife slashed the air in front of my face. She yelled. I was half behind her. I reached with my right hand for her right hand.

The knife stabbed at my arms, slicing my sleeves open, tearing the flesh. Enni was a professional cook. She sharpened her knives herself. I squeezed her wrist. I was surprised by the strength of her arms, her torso. She felt for my left hand on her throat, found a pain point, and squeezed. It felt as if she was tearing my hand off.

I yelled.

Enni struggled.

She turned and jabbed the knife straight at me. I lifted my hand to block it. The blade went through my hand. Enni did what she'd done before — she withdrew the knife. It was a brief movement, but long enough. I leapt forward, aiming for the middle of her body. She swerved sideways and I only half struck her. I got hold of the knife hand and pulled.

We staggered. I wrenched at her hand with all my might. I couldn't get the knife loose. My strength was insufficient, the pain in my left shoulder and right hand seemed to paralyse me.

But Enni fell.

I held onto her wrist with both hands.

A twist.

The knife turned, pointed upward, at the moment we hit the floor, me on my side, Enni on her stomach. The blade sank into her throat.

Enni made a rasping sound.

I got up on my knees. The tip of the knife was poking out of the back of her neck. She thrashed and wheezed, each sound weaker than the last. The knife had gone through the centre of her throat. She stopped moving and lay on the floor, her hair spread out around her head.

On the back of her neck I could see old scars, like long scratches left by fingernails that had tried to tear her neck open.

Wagner thundered on.

I stood up, dripping warm blood on the rug.

OCTOBER — NOVEMBER 2013

The forest was quiet and shadowed, exuding expectation of winter. I held Ketomaa under the arm as we made our way over a tangle of roots. The old man moved slowly and was having particular difficulty with the uneven terrain. The sun peeked out from between the clouds and branches now and then like a kindling fire, and at other times the woods went nearly dark. Our eyes had to try to adjust to the alternating light and shade.

Ketomaa's neck and left cheek were entirely covered in bandages and dressings. The nails had left holes in him. It would take a while for them to scar over. He was pale and weak from his long period of unconsciousness and his stay in the hospital. We were approaching the area the police had excavated.

We hadn't really said anything on the way. Coming to Kalmela had been a joint decision but more instinctive than carefully considered. When he'd woken from the coma I had told him everything I knew, everything I understood. He listened. Then he told me how Henrik Saarinen had tricked him into coming to the abandoned house and wrestled him into submission. When I asked why Saarinen had done it, Ketomaa said he wasn't sure. One reason might be a family relationship that Ketomaa had discovered, one that had begun to dawn on me once my desperate search had come to its end. I'd been blind, but it was understandable.

Ketomaa had been sent home from hospital a few days later. He got in touch with me and said that we should take a little trip if I didn't have any work to do that day. I told him that since a carpenter who'd been recently stabbed not just once but twice wasn't doing much in the way of work, we could go whenever he liked.

Instead of driving into Kalmela, we pulled off a little before the turn and took a narrow dirt road into the forest. It had always looked like just another road winding through the woods and fields around the estate. Now it was impossible to miss; it was like a giant tunnel into an open mouth. The road was filled with the tracks of heavy machinery, an excavator and dumper truck — and of course police cars.

We'd left the car where most of the tyre tracks ended. Ahead there were only the ruts left by the digging equipment.

Ketomaa's breathing was laboured. He stopped. We were close. We would soon reach what we came to see, over the next rise from the look of it.

"Have you been there?" Ketomaa asked. His speech was hard to decipher. He still couldn't move his jaw or cheeks.

"No," I said.

"Do you want to stop here?"

264

"No."

He didn't say any more, and carried on walking. I walked beside him. We came over the rise. We were both panting. If I was sweaty and winded, I could only guess how he must feel. In spite of the wind I loosened my scarf, opened my coat.

A little below us was an area of black earth about the size of a tennis court, tilled and levelled by the excavator. It was quiet. The sun came out from behind the clouds.

"We weren't far off," Ketomaa said, as if guessing my thoughts.

"I suppose not," I said, and looked at him standing beside me. My shoulder hurt, as did my hand.

"In a way we were on the right track all along."

We were about half a kilometre from the shore. The trees had dropped all their leaves. The spruces stood out like bright green spots and the further away they were the more they looked like cut-outs, paper air fresheners stuck onto the grey landscape.

The black patch, the excavated area, was below us. I didn't know what I was looking at. I'd wanted to be here, wanted to see this place. Now I was ready to turn back. The wind blew against my face. I buttoned my coat again.

Ketomaa suddenly lifted his right hand and pressed it against his side, over his kidney.

"Are you all right?" I asked.

"Like a cancer patient with nails shot in him."

"Should we sit down?"

"It will pass."

I edged closer to him, ready to support him if he stumbled.

"I'll ask for help if I need it."

"Of course," I said, and stepped away.

The wind went through my coat. It was the same as it had been up on the ridge, a steady freezing wind going through one layer of clothing, then the next.

"It's actually all just as I thought it would be," Ketomaa said. "Hindsight is easy but sometimes it's all you've got. I read that somewhere."

I had to ask.

"Why did we come here?"

Ketomaa turned and took a moment to focus his blue, wind-moistened eyes on me.

"How does this feel?"

"It's hardly what my mother would have wanted . . ."

"I'm sorry. That's not what I meant," Ketomaa said quietly.

I looked at him. He seemed sincerely sorry. His face looked sad anyway. Or maybe it was just an old man's chilled face.

"I remember something I once heard in the public sauna in Harjutori. There was a man in his fifties whose mother had just died and he came in to take a sauna. When the subject came up, the old guys confessed what a hard time they'd had when their mothers died. Then it got quiet and somebody said: Fathers come and go but you only have one mother."

Ketomaa looked at me. I think we both smiled, as much as the place and the weather allowed.

"I'm sorry for you, of course, but I thought it was important to come here and see what there was to see. That we both see it."

He turned around. I turned too.

There were no cars. Just trees and land. We'd come further than I'd thought.

"What I meant was, how does it feel to stand here, physically," Ketomaa said. "How does it feel in your feet? What if you had to carry an unconscious person, even a light one, up here, and down to that spot, and dig a hole a metre and a half deep?"

He turned again, I did the same, we looked at the black burial site.

"The forest is bulldozed, the land trodden down," he continued. "It's daytime. The sun is shining. And even now, it's hard going. What would it be like in the rain and dark, looking for the path, your feet sinking into the mud, tripping, slipping?"

In profile, Ketomaa looked like an old bird. A long, dry beak, a face shaped by thousands of spells of bad weather.

I remembered Enni's powerful physique, the sharp, quick movements of her hands. Sure, she was as burly as a circus strongwoman, but even she couldn't have done all that. Not even when she was young. Not on a soaking wet, dark October night.

"Even a strong woman couldn't manage it alone," I said. "She would have needed help."

Ketomaa nodded.

"Tanja Metsäpuro's case comes to mind."

"How so?"

"Tanja was carried a long way. There were signs on the body that someone'd had to work hard to tip her into the sea. That was never publicised. It just occurred to me again, standing here."

He took a deep breath.

"And another thing," he said. "Her left earring had been torn out."

"Are those things related?"

He shrugged his thin shoulders.

"Maybe. Who knows."

"You think they are," I said, looking at his furrowed brow and puckered mouth.

"I believe they're both related to the fact that Tanja's case was entirely different from what people thought. The earring, for instance. If someone had wanted to show their strength or demonstrate their cruelty, they would have torn both of them out. I've seen it in more than one case. But only one of Tanja's was removed. And another thing: if you were given a chance to murder someone, would you do it far away from where you planned to hide the body, or would you do it as close as possible to the place you planned to put it, to minimise your risk of getting caught?"

Ketomaa looked at me. His eyes were damp. He wiped them with the back of his glove.

"So, ten years after my mother," I said, continuing his thought, "almost the same pattern. Some woman Henrik Saarinen admires, or falls in love with, or whatever. She disappears. Then the body is found, and both the body and the place indicate that the murderer didn't act alone. We also know that Henrik Saarinen could very well be innocent. Maybe what Saarinen told us was true. All of it. Maybe it means that what happened to Tanja did have something to do with drugs, just as the police suspected. In fact I have reason to believe that drugs were a factor in Henrik Saarinen's inner circle."

Ketomaa nodded. He might have even smiled.

I could see that he was cold. It was time to leave.

"Maybe we really weren't so far off after all," I said, and took his arm, although he tried to protest a little.

OCTOBER — NOVEMBER 2013

Amanda Saarinen's neckline had deepened and widened. Her lipstick was the colour of a ripe cherry just fallen from the tree.

"I'm a little disappointed," she said. "I always thought you were one of those guys who I'd only need to get rid of once."

Her black hair was shining, her breasts pressed up against one another. She folded her hands in her lap and looked as displeased and impatient as you would imagine a restlessly waiting millionaire heiress would be.

"Nice to see you, Amanda."

I sat down across the table from her. The sofa she sat on was shiny and new. It didn't look cheap.

"I'm glad to see you've had a chance to blow your nose," I said.

She looked at me as she would at a pile of old rubbish.

"I know you use cocaine," I said. "But so what? So did Tanja, before she met your father. I'm sure you remember Tanja Metsäpuro, Henrik's girlfriend?"

There was no change in Amanda's expression. Her eyes remained impenetrable and indifferent. I started to wonder if I should be there, with my undeniably flimsy speculations, the way things had taken shape in my mind, fallen into place. The certainty I'd felt on the way was punctured. Doubt flooded through me like cold water. I reminded myself why I'd come. This wasn't over yet.

"Tanja had a bit of a police record at one time," I said. "Nothing serious. Criminal use. It means she was caught using cocaine. The interesting part was who else was charged at the same time. Your husband. Surely you remember."

Amanda smiled. There was nothing friendly about her smile.

"You're all mixed up, Aleksi. I'm sure it's tough to be so alone. I opened my door to you because your mother died. I felt sorry for you, to be blunt."

She put her hands together like a teacher or childminder and leaned forward to indicate that she was getting up, that the lesson or story time, though certainly interesting, was over now. But I was just getting started.

"Amanda, you don't pity anyone. You asked me to kill your father. You opened your door to me because you're scared. And for good reason."

Maybe she was considering this. Or maybe she was just looking at me. Nothing in her face or her eyes told me which. She leaned further forward.

"Who are you? What are you? How dare you?"

I was the caretaker. My mother's son. I'd waited twenty years to do what was right.

"I've sometimes wondered how Henrik met Tanja. It was kind of a surprising attraction, an older millionaire and a single mother the same age as his daughter. It makes you automatically question how they knew each other, where in hell they could have met. Enni's photo album was invaluable in answering that question. I'm sure you know how Enni liked taking photos. It was understandable, since you were her family. In a way."

I took a photo out of my pocket that I'd removed from Enni's album. It was a picture of Henrik Saarinen's yacht, taken sometime in the early 2000s, maybe the summer of 2001 or 2002. Suntanned couples, the hull of the white boat, in the background the sea glittering in the sunlight. I scooted the photo across the table as far as I could reach.

"At first some of these people were strangers to me, of course," I said. "I had to get some assistance from your previous caretaker, the one who was fired. He was happy to help, as I'm sure you can imagine. You know them, of course. That's you and your husband on the left, and another couple on the right: Tanja Metsäpuro and her husband. Cocaine. Not that Henrik knew that. There he is on the right. He met Tanja a few times, and he was smitten. Pretty ironic, isn't it? You practically introduced them."

Amanda leaned back in her chair and put her left leg over her right. She placed her elbow on the armrest and leaned a temple on her fingers. She looked amused.

"Go on," she said.

"I'm almost done."

"And then you'll tell me how much."

"How much what?"

"How much money you want."

272

I shook my head. I looked at her, and I understood something. I would never again lust after a woman like her. I really should have thanked her.

"I've told you before. I don't want your money. I don't want you, and I don't want your money."

"Everybody wants something."

"On that we're in agreement."

"What do you want?"

"I want you to listen and tell me whether I'm right."

"And if I don't?"

"That's up to you. You can listen first and then decide."

She didn't say anything. I took that to mean she was ready to listen. That was enough for me.

"My guess is that quite soon after this photo was taken, after their first meeting, Henrik got in touch with Tanja. Or maybe they met some other way. It doesn't really matter. Tanja divorced her husband. Henrik and Tanja started seeing each other. One day Henrik tells you about their relationship, and naturally it's quite a shock."

Still no reaction.

"You know Tanja from very different circles. You've done coke with her, gone dancing, maybe had a little group sex, as sometimes happens. But you can't tell your father that. You don't like Tanja. The very idea of Tanja, the greedy social climber, infuriates you."

Amanda's face might have flashed a brief sign of life. Maybe a memory. Or maybe she was just annoyed, or bored.

"So you start threatening her," I continued. "Any way you can. Until finally she backs off. It's hard for you to believe such a thing could happen. That there's a person who isn't as greedy, as ruthless as you are. A person who backs off, who gives up. Henrik and Tanja have already broken up, when one evening you and Tanja meet again."

I took a breath. I was coming to the weakest point in my flimsy construction. I was a man trying to round up a herd of wild horses into a pen made of matchsticks.

"Maybe you'd arranged to meet someone there in the car park at the nightclub, or maybe somewhere else. In any case, there you are, and you still hate Tanja, who has the nerve to come to this meeting because she thinks you've both put all that behind you. And there in the car park or wherever, things get out of hand. You're high on coke and maybe you get a little carried away, and you kill Tanja."

Amanda opened her mouth a little, the ripe cherry splitting down the middle as her lips parted.

"All that from one photo," she said. "Congratulations."

I laid my hands down on the arms of the chair. My hot, damp palms felt uncomfortable against the leather, but I left them where they lay. I answered Amanda's gaze and let the comment hang between us. I'd made my way this far across my shaky bridge, and if she was willing to meet me halfway I would gladly wait for her.

"Do you want me to say something?" she asked.

I waved a sweaty hand to indicate encouragement. She flicked her black hair away from her face and smoothed the loose strands into place. Her nails were long and shining.

"Anybody can make up anything they want," she said. "You've had your say. All I'm willing to tell you is that Tanja Metsäpuro wasn't any good at renunciation or struggle. She didn't give anything up."

"And then what?" I said, trying to hide my surprise.

"She wanted her life to go on as before, that's all. She couldn't give anything up. She was the lowest of the low. She didn't understand anything else."

"Unlike you."

"Look at where I live, and look at where she lived."

"Did you have a fight?"

Amanda didn't answer right away. Then she smiled. I'd seen that smile before, on Henrik Saarinen's face. A mocking, superior, almost derisive smile.

"I just had a crazy thought," she said. "I thought you had figured something out, but you haven't. You're Aleksi Kivi, a soon to be unemployed maintenance man, a total loser. As soon as I get my hands on my inheritance, suddenly you're not on the payroll any more. And you can't prove any of this."

"Why is that funny?" I asked, watching as her smile widened.

"You're so close and yet so far off the mark. All you have is your story. We didn't fight. There was nothing to fight about. That whore's earring just got stuck in my coat zipper. Maybe that torn ear made somebody think there'd been an altercation, but that's not what happened. Tanja came to pick up some coke. She was on the wagon for a long time, but then she called this person she knew and said she had to have some. She came to the car park and I saw her and I grabbed a taser."

This person she knew.

I took another reckless step across that rickety bridge, shored up my matchstick fence, but with a surer hand.

"What happened then?"

"Nothing terribly surprising," Amanda said, shrugging her delicate shoulders. Her breasts pressed tight together for a moment. "I got rid of her. But like I said, this is just a chat. You can't prove anything."

"No, of course."

I didn't need to prove anything to anyone. Except myself.

"This little moment is over," Amanda said, putting both feet on the floor again. She braced her hands on her knees so that her shoulders rose up like a wild animal's and the line between her breasts darkened almost to blackness and her face looked hard, shadowless. "I guess you know that this is definitely the last time we'll see each other."

I didn't speak. I got up, glanced towards the bedroom.

I could see the table next to the bed, next to it a chair with a pair of jeans on the back. Men's jeans. Light blue, "distressed". A recognisable style for a man with a deep tan, toned body, gelled hair. I remembered what Ketomaa had told me, the reason Henrik Saarinen had wanted to get rid of him.

I also remembered footwear lying on the floor when I came in the door. Combat boots. The ones I'd seen in that dark garage in Roihupelto.

As these thoughts came together in my mind I remembered other things as well: the meeting on the dock at Kalmela, the loading of the motorboat; that time I heard steps in this apartment from outside the door and no one answered my knocks; what Henrik Saarinen said about Amanda . . .

Someone who can make her give up . . . make her stop . . .

I'd once heard that when a person has an epiphany about a problem he feels as if he's risen above it and can see it all, every bit of it, more clearly than ever before, if only for a moment.

Amanda didn't deserve to be left unaware. I turned. We stood facing each other.

"Say hello to Harmala," I said, "but I'm sure you call him Markus. Tell Markus that I know he was there when my mother was buried, and when Tanja Metsäpuro was killed, or at least when her body was dumped in the sea."

"Like I told you," Amanda said, and stepped closer, close enough that I could smell the perfume that once, a long time ago, had made me tremble in anticipation, excited about what would happen next, aroused. Now it was rancid, revolting. "This is just a little chat. Maybe it happened like you say, or maybe nothing happened the way you think it did. Or it could be anything in between. In any case you can't prove it."

I looked into her icy eyes.

"You lied to me, beat me with a pipe, tried to get me to murder your father. You deserve what you've got. Going to bed every night with your brother."

Still no reaction. At least not on the surface. But I was certain that she'd stopped breathing. Her face was made of stone. She was made of stone.

"Why do you think your father took such a personal interest in hiring an eighteen-year-old?" I said. "He was stuck. Markus is his son. One old policeman figured it out and almost lost his life for it. Henrik didn't want Markus to know, and he couldn't exactly tell you, either, since he knew you were screwing Markus. Of course now that everybody knows about it, it will be clear that Markus is the rightful heir."

I was quiet for a second. Yes, she had stopped breathing, and her icy eyes no longer saw anything.

"Good luck to you both," I said. "You deserve each other."

I left.

I closed the door carefully behind me, pressing it into its frame.

A fury of shrieks could be heard all the way to the street. I was sure I could hear it even as I sped into the traffic on the shore road.

NOVEMBER 2013

"Miia Niemelä."

A voice on the telephone, two words, and I was back where we'd been two months before, when we met in the aisle at the supermarket, me in my ill-fitting, bloody, dirty clothes.

"Hi. It's Aleksi."

"Hi."

"Did I call at a bad time?"

"Sort of. What did you want?"

Noise in the background, people, music.

"I wanted to apologise," I said. "To explain."

"You don't need to explain."

"I disagree. And I know you're still angry at me. That's OK."

"I'm not angry. I don't think about you."

"I think about you. I've thought about you all the time."

The background noise took on a form: a bar, girl-friends, Marvin Gaye, "Sexual Healing". I could picture it all, in fragments: a girls' night out, made-up faces sparkling, dark eyeliner, glossed lips, glasses of wine, tall cocktails, loud talk, laughter, flirtatious glances.

"Wait a minute, all right?"

The noise receded. She was walking. The sound of her heels on the floor reached my ears.

"OK," I heard her say. "I'm out in the lobby. I wanted to tell you that I don't want you to call me."

"I understand. But you once asked me to tell you about myself . . ."

"That was then. Things are different now."

"Do you mean Olli?" I asked, before I could think about it.

"Jesus. You've got a lot of nerve to be jealous six months after leaving me."

I thought I had carefully prepared myself, thought my mind was calm, that I'd got in touch for one reason. I thought I would be altruistic. No matter what happened. No matter what Miia said.

"I'm sorry," I said quickly. "I just wanted to tell you what happened and why I had to do what I did."

"The secret agent."

"What?"

"You sound just like you did back then."

"But I can talk about it now."

"So talk."

"I'm sure it would be better if we could actually meet . . ."

I heard more high heels on the floor, more voices of revellers competing with my anguish.

"It all started when my mother was murdered, twenty years ago," I said, and realised how poorly I had actually prepared. My mind was jumbled with everything I'd been thinking, everything that had happened to me. I knew I should be careful with my words. Luckily neither one of us spoke for a moment.

"Aleksi, I'm sorry, but I've got to ask." Miia's voice was different now, more wary. "Are you serious? I mean, is it true, what you're saying?"

Was it true?

At the very least, it was true.

It was my whole life, up until now.

"Yes. I didn't know how to talk about it. I still don't know. I want you to know how all this happened. Twenty years ago my mother disappeared, and a little while later I found out who killed her."

"Oh Aleksi."

"This is a really long story . . ."

"It's not that."

I waited, didn't rush her. I could hear my heart pounding, the phone line buzzing. A few seconds passed.

"I've just got engaged. Yesterday. I'm out celebrating with friends."

For a moment I didn't know what to say.

I said, "Congratulations."

"Thanks. Aleksi, I'm sorry about what happened to you, to your mother. I'd like to . . . or . . . maybe not right now, since we really . . . But sometime . . ."

I heard a happy shout, music. All of it happening in the same city I was in.

"Maybe sometime," I said, and heard in my mind what I was really saying: *I was a prisoner of my obsession. I did what I had to do, and it tore us apart.*

"Yes, let's," Miia said quietly. "Sometime."

"Yes."

"I mean, it's all right. I was wrong. I'm sorry."

"You have nothing to apologise for. Nothing. See you sometime."

"Yes. Sometime."

NOVEMBER 2013

If you
(kick)
Only knew
(kick)
What I've done
(kick)
For you
(kick)

NOVEMBER 2013

Elias Ahlberg called as I was unpacking boxes. The call was brief: I was to come to his office near Diana Park as soon as possible. I looked around, saw that I only had a few more things left to unpack, stack, move, arrange. How about in half an hour? I asked. Come on over, he said.

Henrik Saarinen's lawyer and former right-hand man had an office on the fourth floor in a hundred-year-old stone building. The meeting room was high-ceilinged and positioned precisely at the level of the treetops. Looking out of the window I felt as if the thin, black, sharp tips of the branches would come through the floor and tickle the soles of my feet like cold, probing fingers. I didn't have long to enjoy the thought before Ahlberg came into the room.

I'd last seen him six months earlier. He was about sixty, greying, in a dark suit that cost about what a small car does. He seemed to be taking my measure again, and still not telling me what it was he was looking for. His merciless blue eyes stared straight at me yet managed to avoid seeming intrusive. You only get good at that after years of practice.

284

"Coffee, tea, juice?" he said, nodding at the thermos, soft drinks, glasses and cups on the table. "Shall we sit down?"

He laid a folder on the table, poured two cups of coffee, and did it all so smoothly that you felt compelled to watch him, even after the coffee was steaming in the cups and one was set in front of me.

"Henrik Saarinen's will," he said, sitting down across from me. "Its final version. You're probably not at all aware of it?"

I shook my head.

"No."

He looked at me a moment longer. The look was neither positive nor negative.

"Henrik changed his will numerous times," Ahlberg said. He opened the folder and looked at the papers, although it was clear that he knew their contents very well. "The most recent change was made just a few days before his death."

That look again, which I returned. I remembered it from my job interview. He was clearly one of those lawyers who also believed in what was between the lines, what was left unsaid.

"This small addition pertains to you. As you know, Henrik Saarinen was a wealthy man. His largest personal holding was of course the investment company that bears his name, Saarinen Capital. Are you familiar with the activity and assets of the company?"

I know everything about them, I thought.

"To some extent, of course," I said, "but I was hired as a caretaker, not a treasurer."

"Quite."

"I mean, I don't know much, but I'm somewhat familiar with it."

"Quite."

The look. A pause.

"The will specifies that upon Henrik Saarinen's death the investment company shall be sold and divided up in the manner designated. In this division of the property you have been allotted a share that is almost exactly 5 per cent."

The look.

"That percentage perhaps sounds small."

A hand stroking smooth paper.

The windows filled with pitch-black, autumn-stripped branches growing up from below.

"The sale is being arranged presently," he continued. "It won't be instantaneous. Some of the holdings are large enough that a buyer has yet to be found. At this point the plan is that the sale should be completed within six months. At that time it will be certain what your portion of the final value will be, but if you wish I can provide an estimate of the value immediately. I remind you, however, that this would only be an estimate, based on the present value of the holdings. Anything could happen, as I'm sure you are aware."

Anything at all definitely could happen.

"May I ask something?"

Ahlberg lowered his right hand with his pen in it onto the table like a surgeon's knife. He leaned slightly back in his chair.

"Naturally. I am at your disposal."

"I'm sorry?"

"According to the will. I'm at your disposal for the duration of the execution of the will."

My turn to look, read between the lines.

"Did Henrik leave anything else?"

"A great deal," Ahlberg said. "The Kalmela estate, of course. Other residences. Some art."

"I mean something like a letter or some kind of message. Something that would tell us more."

Ahlberg shook his head. It was the first movement of its kind of the whole meeting. The first that wasn't absolutely smooth.

"Not to my knowledge," he said.

"Did he say why I was included in the will?"

Head shake. The second of its kind.

"No."

I thought for a moment.

"All right. Who are the other inheritors?"

He found his scalpel again. The pen rose upright, but it didn't make any cuts.

"I can't tell you that."

"Even though you're at my disposal."

"Quite."

He turned his head, looked towards the window, perhaps out of the window.

"A certain portion of the inheritance is already under dispute," he said. "There were some small surprises."

Amanda Saarinen. Markus Harmala.

Lovers. Sister and brother.

Their dispute wouldn't be a short one.

"It doesn't affect your portion in any way," Ahlberg continued. "Your share is precisely defined and unambiguous."

His eyes returned to mine.

"I want to express my condolences for your mother. It's hard to believe such a thing could happen."

I didn't want to talk about it. For twenty years it had driven me. It almost killed me.

"You'll probably get in touch to let me know. About the sale and so on."

"Naturally."

I got up. Ahlberg did the same. Everything was smooth again, businesslike. I came around the table. Ahlberg held out his hand.

"Thank you for your service, Aleksi. I'm sure that Henrik would have said the same."

I took his hand, looked into his eyes. I was ready to leave. Ahlberg, however, didn't let go of my hand. His grip got tighter, or rather warmer, part of that predatory smoothness.

"Aren't you interested in knowing the value of your share?"

I wanted to get away. He sensed this, and let go of my hand.

"If sold at today's prices," he said with a smile — careful, barely perceptible — the first of the meeting — "Almost exactly four million euros."

NOVEMBER 2013

On the red brick wall hung Jesus, on the snow-white coffin glowed a bouquet of red roses. The minister went through the things I'd told him, the organist sat down heavily on his bench.

Thank you for every moment of my life. Thank you for the sunlight and the darkness.

I sat alone in the first row and was a little cold. The wistful light of a November Sunday fell against the brick-covered wall without warming anyone or anything and made it look older.

I didn't know if my mother liked this hymn. We never talked about hymns or funerals. We just lived, we were alive, until suddenly we weren't.

Contrary to what I'd sometimes read or heard, I didn't feel one phase closing and another beginning. It wasn't the end of the old or the start of the new.

Just the opposite.

Everything continued. Life continued.

I would live. I would remember.

I didn't feel any particular satisfaction in the fact that the person responsible for my mother's death was dead. The dead don't know anything about their punishment. Only the living can carry a thing with them.

I remembered and I always would remember.

Maybe that's what memory is for. To give us a life when it's been taken away from us.

My mother would exist as long as I remembered her in thousands of images, moments, words that weren't images or moments or words as the world would understand them.

For twenty years I had tried to adjust to the idea that my mother was dead and gone.

Only to realise that she existed as long as I did, in every day of my life, one of which would be my last.

I no longer wondered what she would have said to me if she'd known that her time was up, if she'd known what would happen when she went down those stairs, opened that door and got into that car.

Everything had been said.

Everything was clear.

She had given me my life, she had done her best, she had made a mistake. That's how a person's life is. We don't achieve what we reach for. We get dirty, get broken, drown. If we don't bury someone else with us, we can be content.

My mother once said that I could be anything I wanted to be.

It wasn't true. Not then, and not now.

But it was important that she said it. That tells me everything — how much she loved me, believed in me, believed I could change the course of fate.

Rays of sunlight struck my mother's coffin.

Life hurts, and is over in an instant.

As the hymn played, something made me turn my head and look behind me.

Ketomaa should have been the only other mourner here, but far behind him, in the very last row next to the door sat a dark-haired man whose face I couldn't quite make out. He looked outwardly as if he'd come to the right place — black suit, dark blue or black tie, white shirt. He didn't seem to notice anyone looking at him. He didn't move at all, and I could only assume that he was gazing straight ahead.

I didn't recognise him but there was something familiar about him. I searched out Ketomaa's eyes and tried to get him to turn and look. He didn't, and I let it go.

The hymn ended. The service was over. I got up and turned around. The man had disappeared. Ketomaa gave me a questioning look. My face must have showed my bafflement. The chapel hummed with emptiness. I shrugged.

I didn't know why I felt the way I did.